Son of Afghanistan

An Afsar Ramos Thriller

DAVID L. PRESTON

Copyright © 2025 David L Preston

All Rights Reserved

ISBN:
Paperback 978-1-966890-05-8
eBook 978-1-966890-04-1

Azalea City Publishing, LLC
Mobile, AL 36693
www.azaleacitypublishing.com
Cover design: Artillery Design Company Ltd
https://www.artillerydesign.co

DAVIDLPRESTON.COM

OTHER WORKS BY DAVID:

Unknown Soldier: World War 1

1828

The Killer Family: A Martello Family Thriller

DEDICATION

To Mom, this book brought up feelings I didn't even know I was suppressing. Even though I never got the chance to know you, I feel like you are watching over me still.

ACKNOWLEDGEMENTS

To the reviewers whose input helped to make this story better, thank you. Brian Lambrecht, Paula Webb, Deza'Rae Collins, and Mary Palmer.

Prologue

2002

The morning heat already clung to the air like a heavy wool blanket as Corporal Jack Ramos leaned over a battered folding table inside the operations tent at Forward Operating Base Salerno. A laminated map of the Khost Province was spread out in front of him, weighed down by a coffee mug, a stray ammo magazine, and a half-eaten protein bar.

His squad, a rough collection of Marines and Army attachments, lounged around the tent. Helmets sat loose on the floor, rifles rested against the walls, and a few of the guys were still rubbing the sleep from their eyes. The mood was easy, almost lazy — just another routine patrol, another walk in the dirt.

Ramos tapped the map twice with his pen, drawing everyone's attention. "Alright, listen up, ladies," he said, a grin tugging at the corner of his mouth. "Today's big adventure is another scenic tour of beautiful downtown Spera. No red carpets, no paparazzi, and — fingers crossed — no fireworks."

A few of the guys chuckled. Private First Class Dawson, the baby of the group with a mess of blonde hair under his helmet, raised his hand like a kid in school.

"Sir, any chance the locals throw in free chai this time? Last time they gave us water that tasted like it came out of a donkey trough."

"Negative, Dawson," Ramos said, pretending to consult his notes. "Today's menu is strictly donkey trough. Hydrate accordingly."

More laughs. Even Sergeant Hernandez, who normally wore a permanent scowl, cracked a grin.

Ramos straightened up and pointed at the map again, the pen tracing a path along the main road through Spera.

"We'll move out in two squads — Alpha and Bravo. Bravo takes the southern route through the bazaar. Alpha — that's us — will skirt the northern edge, swing by that busted water pump the engineers flagged last week."

He paused and looked around the tent, making sure he still had their attention.

"Rules of engagement stay the same. Eyes open, heads on a swivel. We are not expecting any contact, but we treat every patrol like it's live until we're back behind these walls. Anyone sees something funky — you speak up. Don't be a hero."

Sergeant Hernandez chimed in from the corner.

"Copy that. No one plays John Wayne today."

"Exactly," Ramos nodded. "We're in and out. Back in time for lunch and more MREs that taste like salted sand."

A round of mock groans filled the tent. Dawson leaned back in his chair.

"Man, I heard Alpha Company over at Bagram got a shipment of real pizza last week. Why do they get all the luck?"

"Because the Army hates us," Specialist Tran deadpanned from the other side of the tent.

Ramos let the laughter settle before clapping his hands together.

"Alright, mount up in twenty. Final gear check in fifteen. Let's make this quick and painless."

The squad started moving, gathering their gear with the lazy urgency of men who didn't expect trouble but knew better than to slack off completely. Ramos stayed behind for a moment, staring down at the map, a little knot of unease tightening in his gut.

It was probably nothing.

Probably just another boring patrol.

Still, he tapped the laminated surface once more for luck before grabbing his rifle and stepping out into the bright Afghan morning.

The sun was already climbing higher by the time the squad loaded up into the dusty green MRAPs lined up outside the ops tent. Their heavy doors slammed shut with metallic thuds, each echoing through the compound like warning bells no one paid much attention to anymore.

Ramos climbed into the front passenger seat of the lead vehicle, tossing his rifle into the rack before pulling his seatbelt tight with a practiced yank. He adjusted his helmet, flipping his visor down just as Sergeant Hernandez slid behind the wheel, grumbling under his breath about the heat.

"AC's busted again," Hernandez said, banging the dashboard like that might magically fix it.

"Good thing we love the weather here," Ramos replied with a smirk. "Sweat builds character."

In the back, Dawson, Tran, and Specialist Keller were settling in, helmets bobbing as the MRAP's heavy engine rumbled to life.

"You sure this thing's not gonna die on us halfway there?" Keller asked, patting the armored wall beside him.

"Faith, Keller," Tran said dryly. "Faith and duct tape."

The convoy of three MRAPs rolled out of FOB Salerno, rumbling past the Hesco barriers and guard towers. The gates creaked open, and the Afghan countryside yawned wide in front of them — dry hills, scraggly trees, dust clouds chasing the horizon.

Inside the cab, the radio crackled with chatter from the other vehicles.

"Bravo One to Alpha One — race you there," came the voice of Sergeant Price from the second MRAP, his tone playful.

"Copy that, Bravo One," Ramos said, smiling as he keyed the mic. "Winner gets first pick of the hot chow... if there's anything edible left."

More laughter across the net.

The MRAPs bounced along the rough dirt roads, kicking up massive trails of dust behind them.

Occasionally, Ramos would catch glimpses of small villages tucked into the hills, little knots of mud-brick homes and fields stitched with struggling green.

"Hey, Corporal," Dawson called from the back. "You ever think about what you're gonna do when you get out? I'm thinking... beach bar in Florida. Flip-flops, cold beer. No body armor."

Ramos glanced over his shoulder.

"Sounds nice. You got the money for that dream, Private?"

"Not yet," Dawson said, grinning. "But I'm gonna marry rich."

"You better hope she's blind and doesn't mind the smell," Hernandez said without missing a beat.

The road curved south, and the ridgelines closed in a little tighter. Ramos scanned the hills automatically, his mind half on the terrain, half on the casual banter behind him.

No one really expected trouble today.

It was supposed to be quiet.

Just another routine patrol through Spera.

But even as he chuckled at another wisecrack from the backseat, that same tight knot from earlier twisted just a little harder in Ramos' gut.

He shifted in his seat, the MRAP rattling over a deep rut in the road and tried to shake it off.

The convoy slowed as they approached the edge of Spera, the small village clustered at the base of a rocky hillside. Children darted between low stone walls, dusty sheep wandered across the narrow roads, and the air was thick with the smell of wood smoke and livestock.

Hernandez eased the MRAP to a halt just outside the village's main thoroughfare. The other two vehicles pulled in behind them in a loose staggered formation, engines idling low like patient beasts.

"Alright, ladies and gentlemen," Ramos said, unbuckling and grabbing his rifle. "You know the drill. Standard two-by-two formation. Stay frosty, stay polite."

"Roger that," Keller said, already checking the radio strapped to his vest.

The doors of the MRAPs swung open with heavy groans, and the squad spilled out into the sunlight, boots crunching against the dry dirt. Without a word, they fanned out into their familiar pattern — two columns, spaced just right for visibility and cover, weapons low but ready.

It was automatic by now, like muscle memory.

Ramos took point on the left side, Tran sliding into position opposite him. Behind them, Keller and Dawson filled the gaps, scanning rooftops and alleys out of pure instinct. The rest of the platoon broke into similar formations behind them, their discipline smooth, almost lazy.

A few villagers glanced up from their morning routines — old men sitting cross-legged in front of shops, women carrying baskets of goods on their heads. Most barely spared them a second look. They were used to the Americans passing through.

"Man, it's like we're part of the scenery now," Dawson muttered under his breath, adjusting his sunglasses.

"Good," Ramos said quietly. "Means nobody's nervous."

They moved deeper into the village, following the narrow street that cut through its center. The same broken-down pickup truck sat in front of the same tiny tea shop, the same old man chewing on a toothpick under the faded awning. A goat trotted lazily across the path, forcing Keller to sidestep it with a grunt.

"Watch out, Special Forces," Tran teased him. "Goat's got a mean look."

"Ha, ha," Keller replied dryly, giving the animal a wide berth.

The squad kept moving, eyes sharp but posture relaxed. It was easy to slip into the rhythm of it — steady steps, slow turns at intersections, scanning windows and doorways without really thinking about it.

In the distance, Ramos spotted the small plaza where they usually paused to hand out water bottles and basic supplies, a goodwill gesture the villagers had come to expect.

He keyed his mic.

"First hold point coming up. Standard setup. Keller, Dawson, you're on security. Hernandez, get the goodwill packs ready."

"Roger that," came the replies, crisp and casual.

Ramos glanced up at the clear blue sky, the heat pressing down like a heavy hand, and for a moment he let himself believe it really would be just another boring patrol.

He should've known better.

The squad was only a few dozen meters from the plaza when the first shout pierced the heavy morning air.

A sharp, desperate cry — a woman's voice.

Ramos froze mid-step, his head snapping toward the noise. Down a narrow side street to their right, a figure burst into view — a young woman, sprinting barefoot, her long shawl flapping wildly behind her. Hot on her heels were three men, shouting in Pashto, brandishing thick wooden clubs above their heads.

"The hell—?" Dawson muttered, raising his rifle instinctively but keeping it pointed down.

The villagers nearby didn't react — they simply lowered their eyes or turned their backs, pretending not to see.

Ramos clicked his mic. "Eyes on! Right side, one female, three male aggressors. No obvious firearms."

Keller, already shifting his stance, said under his breath, "Looks like a public beating about to happen."

"Doesn't mean it's none of our business," Ramos said firmly.

The woman stumbled, catching herself just before she hit the dirt. The lead man swung his club in a brutal arc, just missing her shoulder.

"Contact front! Move!" Ramos barked.

Without waiting for a formal order, the squad pivoted as one, their formation rippling like a well-oiled machine. Tran and Dawson peeled right to cover the narrow mouth of the alley, while Keller and Hernandez spread out to create a perimeter, blocking any interference from onlookers.

Ramos stepped forward, rifle ready but still angled low — a clear show of force without escalating things immediately. "HEY!" he shouted, voice cutting through the commotion. "Stop!"

The three men skidded to a halt, startled. One of them turned and barked something harsh in Pashto, pointing at the woman.

Ramos raised a hand, palm outward.

"Back off. Now."

The woman, panting hard, darted behind Ramos, clutching the back of his vest like a lifeline. Her dark eyes were wide with terror.

"Sir?" Keller called from his flank, tense. "We got movement — curious eyes gathering."

Ramos nodded without looking. "Hold your sectors. I'll handle this."

The tallest of the three men took a step forward, club still raised, shouting furiously. Ramos caught a few words — *dishonor, punishment, family.*

Tran, from the corner of his mouth:

"Sounds like an honor beating, Sir."

"I figured," Ramos muttered back grimly.

The villagers were starting to cluster at the edges of the plaza, forming a wide, uncertain circle. Ramos could feel the weight of their stares — silent, expectant, waiting to see what the Americans would do.

Ramos squared his shoulders and took another step forward, cutting the distance between him and the aggressors. He kept his voice calm but loud enough to carry.

"This woman is under our protection now. Back away and there won't be any trouble."

The lead man snarled something guttural, something Ramos didn't catch — but the posture was universal: defiance.

The three raised their clubs again, this time edging forward with more purpose.

Keller shifted his weight, his rifle subtly rising. "Say the word, boss."

Ramos narrowed his eyes, every muscle coiling for a fight — "Tran, get up here!" Ramos barked without taking his eyes off the three angry men.

Tran hustled over, lowering his rifle but keeping his other hand near his sidearm. He stood close to the woman, speaking in low, careful Pashto. She rattled off a stream of words, her voice trembling but steady enough to be understood.

Tran frowned deeply as he translated, keeping his voice just loud enough for Ramos to hear.

"She says... they're her uncles and brother. They claim she dishonored the family by getting pregnant. They are gonna kill her to 'restore honor.'"

Ramos felt his stomach twist in disgust.

The lead man shouted something again — sharp, accusing. His grip on the club tightened.

"Yeah, screw that," Ramos muttered. He clicked his radio. "Hernandez, run back to the MRAPs. Bring 'em here now. Double time."

"Roger that!" Hernandez barked back.

Turning back to the squad, Ramos raised his voice just enough for his team to hear but not provoke the growing crowd. "Form up. Watch the perimeter. We're pulling out, we're taking her with us."

The squad tightened up instantly, weapons at low ready, eyes scanning the villagers closing in at the edges of the street. Tension crackled in the air.

Tran gently guided the young woman behind Ramos, shielding her with his body. "She's scared but she's willing to come," he said.

"Good," Ramos grunted.

In the distance, the low, familiar rumble of engines broke the heavy silence. A moment later, the two MRAPs came screeching into view, tires kicking up clouds of dust. Hernandez leaned out the side window, waving frantically.

"Mount up!" Ramos shouted.

The squad moved as one. Dawson and Keller jogged backward toward the vehicles, covering the retreat, while Tran practically lifted the young woman into the back of the nearest MRAP. Ramos kept his rifle up until the last second, locking eyes with the furious men still frozen in the alley, their clubs twitching in their fists.

"You wanna try me?" Ramos growled under his breath.

None of them moved.

Satisfied, Ramos backed into the MRAP and slammed the door behind him. The heavy vehicle lurched forward immediately, engines roaring as the convoy peeled away from Spera.

Inside the rattling MRAP, Ramos finally let out a breath and turned to the young woman. She was huddled in a corner seat, staring at him with wide, cautious eyes.

He offered her a small, tired smile.

"You're safe now," he said, his voice softer. "What's your name?"

The young woman hesitated for a moment, then spoke in accented but clear English.

"Afsoon."

Ramos nodded, memorizing it. "Afsoon," he repeated, locking eyes with her. "You're gonna be okay."

As the MRAPs sped toward the distant safety of Forward Operating Base Salerno, the dust of Spera swallowed the angry shouts fading behind them.

Chapter 1

Afsar Ramos had always stood out in a crowd, though he never intended to. At six-foot-one, he carried himself with a quiet, almost unassuming confidence. His dark Afghan complexion, a deep olive brown that spoke to his roots, contrasted sharply with the paler tones of the university campus around him. Thick black hair, usually combed neatly to the side, framed a face marked by high cheekbones, a strong jaw, and intelligent brown eyes that seemed to absorb everything around them.

He was fit — the kind of fit that came from discipline rather than vanity. His frame filled out his clothes naturally, a product of consistent early-morning runs, not endless hours spent posing in a gym mirror. Broad shoulders, a straight back, and quick, purposeful movements completed the picture of a man who took himself — and everything he did — seriously.

Afsar was a Senior at Middle Tennessee State University, majoring in International Relations. Where some students ambled through their education, switching majors like changing shirts, Afsar had known exactly what he wanted from the start. His professors described him as sharp, insightful, and relentless in debate — always respectful but never one to back down from a challenge. He approached academics the same way he approached the rest of his life: with a strict adherence to routine and structure.

Every morning began the same way: up at 5:30 a.m., a three-mile run before breakfast, a quick review of his daily planner over black coffee, and then off to his classes or the library. Even his weekends followed a schedule that most of his friends found exhausting just to hear about. But Afsar didn't mind. Routine gave him stability, a sense of control in a world that often felt chaotic. It kept him grounded, focused, and ready for whatever came next.

Afsar tugged open the heavy glass doors of the Student Recreation Center, letting in a burst of spring air behind him. He adjusted the strap of his gym bag over his shoulder, his sneakers squeaking slightly on the polished floor. As he stepped inside, he immediately noticed the buzz of activity — louder, more chaotic than usual.

Rows of folding tables had been set up across the basketball courts, manned by student volunteers in matching t-shirts. Banners hung from the rafters, announcing something about a campus-wide job fair. Students clustered around the tables, their voices echoing off the lofty ceilings, brochures and flyers flapping in their hands.

Afsar barely spared it a glance.

Some kind of event, he thought, weaving his way through the crowd with the natural efficiency of someone used to tuning out distractions.

"Hey, man, you looking for a summer internship?" a kid in a blue shirt called out, waving a glossy pamphlet.

Afsar gave a polite shake of his head. "No thanks. Got it covered," he said, his voice calm, measured.

He continued on toward the weight room at the back of the center, the sounds of the crowd fading into the background. He had a schedule to keep. Midday workouts weren't optional — they were as much a part of his day as breathing. Besides, he found comfort in the rhythmic clank of weights and the controlled atmosphere of the gym, far from the noise and unpredictability of the main floor.

Afsar slid into the locker room, tossed his bag onto a bench, and began changing with the same focused routine he'd followed all year.

Afsar moved smoothly through his workout, headphones in, the music pounding a steady rhythm in his ears. Bench press, pull-ups, squats — everything on his program, no deviations. His muscles burned in a familiar, reassuring way, each rep clearing his mind of everything but focus.

Still, even as he worked through his routine, part of his mind kept drifting back to the career fair he'd walked past. It was unusual for him to break from his schedule, but something about it tugged at him. Maybe it was the timing. Senior year was slipping away faster than he liked to admit, and the future was no longer something abstract — it was waiting just around the corner.

He racked the weights after his last set, wiped down the bench, and grabbed his water bottle. As he toweled off, he caught sight of himself in the mirror — dark skin still flushed from exertion, black hair damp with sweat, his lean six-foot-one frame showing the definition he'd worked hard for but never obsessed over. Fit, but not the gym-rat type. Just strong enough.

Maybe it's time to start thinking a step ahead, he thought, tossing his towel into the hamper.

He shrugged back into his jeans and a plain black t-shirt, slinging his backpack over one shoulder. On his way out of the locker room, he caught himself smirking — a rare break from routine. Professor Howard would probably have a heart attack if he heard.

As he stepped back into the bustling main hall, Afsar scanned the crowd. Sure enough, he spotted the familiar green and gold signage of the U.S. Army booth tucked along the far wall. Two recruiters in pressed dress uniforms stood behind the table, talking animatedly with a group of students.

Afsar took a deep breath, adjusted the strap of his backpack, and started weaving his way toward them.

Afsar moved steadily through the crowd; his gaze locked on the Army table. Students weaved past him, some clutching brochures, others animatedly talking to recruiters or friends. His plan was simple — stop by, grab some information, maybe set up a follow-up meeting. Quick and efficient, just the way he liked things.

But then he felt it — that almost physical sensation of being watched.

He glanced to his left and caught the eyes of a woman standing behind a booth draped in deep blue cloth, decorated with the sleek, unmistakable seal of the Central Intelligence Agency. Her stare was sharp, focused, almost clinical — but not unkind. Like she was sizing him up and already knew something about him he hadn't said aloud.

Without thinking, Afsar slowed to a stop in front of her table.

"Good afternoon," the woman said, her voice calm and measured, with just a hint of a friendly smile. She wore a dark blazer over a powder blue blouse, and her ID badge simply read *Ambar Shoeston*. "I'm Ambar

Shoeston. I represent the Directorate of Operations at the CIA. Are you interested in hearing about some career opportunities?"

Afsar blinked, thrown off balance for a moment. This hadn't been part of the plan. Still, he found himself answering, "Uh, sure. Why not?"

Ambar's smile widened slightly, and she gestured to a set of meticulously organized pamphlets on the table. "Most people think the CIA only hires analysts who sit behind desks," she said. "But we have a wide range of career paths — operations officers, paramilitary specialists, cyber operatives, linguists, and more. Some positions are field-oriented, others are more strategic. We look for people who can think critically, adapt under pressure, and who thrive in environments where structure isn't always guaranteed."

She watched him carefully as she spoke, as if studying his reactions.

Afsar nodded slowly, feeling curiosity spark in his chest despite himself. "And, uh... you recruit straight out of college?"

"We do," Ambar confirmed. "We have programs for seniors and graduate students. If you're serious about serving your country but want a different kind of challenge..." She let the sentence hang, letting the weight of her words sink in.

Afsar glanced over his shoulder at the Army booth —
still there, still an option. But something about
Ambar's calm intensity, about the air of mystery she
carried, held him in place.

He turned back to her, raising an eyebrow. "Okay,"
he said, the corner of his mouth twitching upward.
"You've got my attention."

Ambar's eyes gleamed slightly, almost imperceptibly,
as she leaned a little closer across the table,
maintaining her casual, approachable demeanor.

"So, Afsar," she said, rolling his name naturally off her
tongue, "where are you from?"

"Water Valley," Afsar replied easily, shifting his
backpack higher on his shoulder. "It's a small town
here in Tennessee. You probably haven't heard of it."

Ambar chuckled softly. "Try me. I've been to plenty
of small towns most people can't find on a map."

Afsar smirked a little but shrugged. "Well, it's pretty
rural. Not much to it. I grew up there with my mom
and dad. She passed away a few years back."

"I'm sorry to hear that," Ambar said, her tone
softening just a fraction. "Was she from around there
too?"

Afsar shook his head. "No, she was Afghan. Came to the U.S. before I was born. Met my dad while he was stationed overseas." His voice dipped slightly with the memory, but he kept his expression steady.

Ambar nodded thoughtfully, her instincts sharpening. "Did she teach you any languages growing up?"

"Yeah," Afsar said, a little surprised at the question. "She made sure I could speak Dari fluently. I'm conversational in Pashto too, and my Farsi is... almost native level. Mom was pretty insistent about it."

For the first time, Ambar's polished, recruiter mask cracked ever so slightly, revealing a flash of genuine intrigue. She tilted her head, studying him with renewed interest.

"That's impressive," she said, her voice low, almost conspiratorial. "Not many people can say that. Especially not at your age."

Afsar chuckled modestly. "It's just how I grew up. It didn't seem like a big deal at the time."

"Trust me," Ambar said, her eyes locking onto his with new intensity, "it's a very big deal."

There was a brief pause between them, the sounds of the busy career fair fading into background noise for a moment. Afsar felt a strange electricity in the air — like the ground had shifted slightly under his feet, and he was standing at the edge of something he couldn't quite see yet.

Ambar leaned casually against the table; her posture relaxed but purposeful. "Let me explain something real quick before you head over to the Army table," she said, catching the faint glance Afsar had thrown in that direction.

Afsar gave a polite nod, folding his arms across his chest, prepared to listen but clearly signaling that his mind was still elsewhere.

"The Agency's Afghanistan directorate operates a little differently than what most people think," Ambar began, her voice low and deliberate. "We need people who can blend in—not just Americans who look the part, but people who *are* the part. People who understand the culture, the language, the instincts. People who can read a situation before it even happens."

She paused, letting her words hang in the air for a second longer than necessary.

"You fit a profile that's extremely rare, Afsar," she continued, her tone almost persuasive now. "You were born here, you're American, but you carry the understanding of another world. That's the kind of asset that can make all the difference."

Afsar listened respectfully, nodding slightly but keeping his expression guarded. He appreciated the attention, but he wasn't looking for a new direction—not today, anyway. His plan was set. Finish school. Talk to the Army. Serve his country in a way he had envisioned for years.

"Thanks," he said, his voice even. "I appreciate you taking the time to talk with me. But I really should check out the Army recruiters before they pack up."

Ambar smiled, undeterred. She reached into a small stack of folders behind her and pulled out a simple, nondescript card.

"I understand," she said smoothly, holding out the card between two fingers. "But if you don't mind, I'd love to get your contact information. Just so we can stay in touch. You never know where life will take you."

Afsar hesitated for a moment, then, figuring there was no harm, scribbled his email and phone number on the card she handed him.

"Thanks, Afsar," Ambar said warmly, tucking the card away. "We'll be in touch."

Afsar nodded once, offering a polite smile, and turned, weaving his way through the crowd toward the Army table—unaware that a door had quietly opened behind him, one he hadn't even intended to knock on.

***

2010

The tires hummed against the cracked pavement as the old Dodge truck rumbled down the narrow country road. Afsar sat in the passenger seat, his small legs dangling just above the floorboard, nervously kicking back and forth. He clutched his worn backpack tightly in his lap, glancing up at his father every few seconds.

Jack Ramos gripped the steering wheel harder than necessary, his knuckles pale against the dark leather. His jaw was set tight, and deep lines carved across his forehead beneath the shadow of his ballcap. He stared straight ahead, his lips pressed together in a thin, grim line. Even at eight years old, Afsar could tell something was very wrong.

"Dad?" Afsar piped up; his voice was tentative. "Is Mom gonna be okay?"

Jack blinked hard, as if snapping out of some deep, heavy thought. He glanced over at his son for just a second, forcing a small smile that didn't reach his worried eyes.

"She's tough, buddy," Jack said, voice rough. "Your mom's the toughest woman I ever met. She's just... she's just gotta rest a little, that's all."

Afsar nodded, trying to believe him, but the tightness in his father's voice made his stomach twist into knots. He turned his gaze out the window, watching the fields blur past, the occasional farmhouse standing solemn against the grey afternoon sky.

"Can we bring her the drawing I made?" Afsar asked, pulling a folded piece of paper from his backpack.

Jack finally allowed himself a real smile, brief but genuine. He reached over and ruffled Afsar's thick black hair.

"Yeah, bud. She'll love that. Might even frame it and put it right next to her bed," he said, clearing his throat afterward like he was trying to push down something heavier.

The hospital wasn't far now. Afsar could see the dull brick building rising up at the edge of town, its windows dark and heavy-looking, like tired eyes.

Jack's face tightened again as they pulled into the small parking lot, his hands momentarily frozen on the keys before he twisted them out of the ignition.

He sat there for a second, staring at the dashboard, his breathing slow and heavy.

Afsar sat still, watching him. "Dad?"

Jack finally turned, putting a strong but trembling hand on Afsar's shoulder.

"Listen, kiddo," he said quietly. "When we go in there... you just talk to her like normal, okay? Tell her about your day, your schoolwork. Tell her about that big test you got an 'A' on. She'll like that. Just... keep her smiling."

Afsar nodded solemnly. "I can do that."

Jack gave his shoulder a gentle squeeze, then opened his door with a grunt. "Alright then. Let's go see your mama."

Together, they stepped out of the truck, Afsar clutching his drawing tightly as they made their way toward the heavy glass doors of the hospital.

The automatic doors gave a low whoosh as Jack and Afsar stepped into the hospital's sterile, cold-smelling lobby. The fluorescent lights buzzed overhead, and a nurse behind the front desk offered them a polite, tired smile.

Jack gave a quick nod but didn't stop. He knew the way by heart now.

Afsar trotted alongside him, the soles of his sneakers squeaking lightly against the polished tile. His small hand occasionally brushed against Jack's calloused one, but he didn't grab it — he was trying to be brave, like his dad.

They moved through long, pale-blue hallways lined with faded posters about handwashing and flu season. Jack kept his eyes forward, his boots echoing quietly in the nearly empty hall.

"Is she still in Room 112?" Afsar asked in a whisper, as if afraid speaking too loud might somehow make things worse.

"Yeah, buddy. Same room," Jack replied without looking down.

When they reached Room 112, Jack paused for a second outside the door, his hand hovering just over the handle. He drew a slow breath in through his nose and out through his mouth. Then he pushed it open gently.

The room was dim, the only light coming from a small bedside lamp. Machines beeped softly in the background, and the air smelled faintly of antiseptic mixed with something sweeter — probably the flowers on the nightstand.

Afsoon lay in the bed, her skin pale against the white sheets. Her long black hair was braided over one shoulder, and her chest rose and fell in slow, shallow breaths. She looked so small compared to how Afsar always remembered her — strong, lively, smiling.

Jack motioned silently to the chairs by the window, and Afsar followed him over, sitting down carefully. He placed his drawing on his lap and stared at his mother, willing her to open her eyes.

Jack sat heavily beside him, elbows on his knees, his face cradled in his hands for a long moment before he looked up at Afsoon again. His fingers tapped nervously against his thigh, but he didn't say a word.

Minutes ticked by.

Afsar swung his feet slowly under the chair, glancing between his dad and his sleeping mom, the weight of the room pressing down on him.

"She looks tired," Afsar whispered, his voice barely audible.

"Yeah," Jack murmured. "She's fighting hard, though. Just like always."

Afsar nodded, hugging the drawing to his chest. He decided right then he'd tell her about everything — the spelling test, the book report, even the frog he found by the creek yesterday. He wanted her to have reasons to smile when she woke up.

Jack reached over and gently tousled Afsar's hair again, a silent thank you for just being there, for being strong.

And then — a soft sound, a faint sigh — and Afsoon's eyelids fluttered open.

Jack immediately rose from his chair when he saw her stir, crossing the room in two quick strides. He crouched by the bed, his hand gently wrapping around hers.

"Hey, sweetheart," Jack said softly, his voice catching a little. "It's me. I'm here. Afsar's here too."

Afsoon's eyes, still heavy with exhaustion, flickered to life at the mention of her son. Her lips parted in a faint, cracked whisper.

"Afsar... come here, jaanam," she said, barely above a breath, but the love and warmth in her voice filled the room.

Afsar scrambled out of his chair, clutching his drawing tightly. He hesitated for only a second before carefully climbing up onto the bed, mindful of the tubes and wires. Jack helped guide him gently, making sure he didn't tug anything accidentally.

Afsoon opened her arms weakly, and Afsar nestled against her side, resting his head carefully on her shoulder.

"I brought you something," Afsar said, holding up the crumpled piece of paper.

Afsoon smiled — a soft, weary smile — and with Jack's help, she unfolded it. It was a drawing of their family: Afsar, Jack, and Afsoon, all standing in front of a house, the sun beaming overhead.

"It's beautiful," she whispered, tracing her finger lightly over the stick figures. "Just like you."

Afsar beamed, then quickly launched into all the things he had saved up to tell her: how he got a ninety-five on his spelling test, how he was reading a book about space, and how he found a frog by the creek yesterday that tried to jump into his shoe.

Afsoon laughed — a thin, almost soundless laugh — but the joy was still there, shining in her tired eyes.

"You are so smart," she said, brushing a trembling hand through his hair. "So brave."

Afsar leaned closer, his little hand resting over hers.

"Don't be afraid, jaanam," she whispered, her voice suddenly steady despite her frailness. "You are special, Afsar. You're meant for something greater."

Afsar blinked up at her, his young mind not fully understanding, but feeling the weight and importance of her words deep in his chest.

Jack stood quietly at the side of the bed, watching the two most important people in his world, his jaw tight with emotion.

Afsoon's fingers gently squeezed Afsar's hand, as if willing her strength into him.

"Promise me you'll remember," she said, her breath growing lighter. "Promise me."

Afsar nodded solemnly, clutching her hand tighter. "I promise, Mama."

After a few more minutes of quiet conversation, Jack gently urged Afsar to say goodbye, knowing that they needed to leave before the visiting hours ended. Afsar reluctantly leaned in and kissed his mother's forehead, pressing his small hand to her cheek one last time.

"I'll be back soon, Mama," Afsar whispered.

Afsoon gave a weak smile, her hand lingering on his as he pulled away.

"Be good," she whispered. "Take care of your papa."

Jack nodded, wiping away a tear that had escaped down his cheek. He gave his wife one final lingering look before turning to Afsar.

"Come on, son. It's time to go," Jack said, his voice thick with emotion.

The two of them made their way out of the room, Jack's arm around Afsar's shoulder. As they exited the hospital, the fluorescent lights seemed almost too bright after the dim, sterile quiet of the room.

Outside, the cool evening air greeted them, a slight breeze carrying the scent of the city. Jack led Afsar to the truck, and they climbed in together. Afsar sat quietly, gazing out the window, the weight of the visit pressing on his young shoulders. Jack started the truck, and they began the drive back to Water Valley.

The drive was quiet, the rhythmic hum of the tires on the asphalt filling the silence. Afsar was lost in thought, thinking about his mother's words. He didn't fully understand them yet, but they lingered with him like an unspoken promise.

As they neared the outskirts of town, Jack's phone buzzed on the dashboard. He glanced at it and picked it up, answering quickly.

"Jack," the voice on the other end said. "We need you back at the hospital. There's been an incident. It's your wife… Afsoon's... We lost her."

The words hit Jack like a punch to the gut. He didn't say anything at first, just stared ahead through the windshield, the road stretching out before him, blurring. His grip tightened on the wheel as he felt a sudden, sharp pain in his chest.

"Jack? Are you there?" the voice asked again, concerned.

Jack slowly pulled the truck over to the side of the road, his body frozen in place. He closed his eyes and bowed his head, the weight of the news crushing him. He took a shaky breath, trying to steady himself. The sound of his breathing seemed too loud in the truck as his heart hammered painfully against his ribcage.

Afsar, sitting quietly in the passenger seat, glanced over at his father. "Dad? What's wrong?"

Jack didn't respond at first. The weight of what he had just learned, the devastation that had just hit him, was too much to bear. After a long moment, he finally managed to speak.

"She's gone, Afsar," he said, his voice barely a whisper. "Your mom... she's gone."

Afsar's eyes widened as he turned to face his father, confusion and fear in his gaze. "But... but I just saw her. She... she can't be gone."

Jack didn't have the words to explain. Instead, he simply sat there, his head bowed in sorrow, unable to speak as tears welled in his eyes.

The road ahead seemed endless now, and the future was suddenly uncertain.

Chapter 2

Ambar Shoeston watched Afsar Ramos weave through the thinning crowd, his focus now fixed on the U.S. Army table at the far end of the career fair. She didn't call out to stop him. She didn't need to. Her instincts, sharp as a scalpel after more than a decade in the intelligence community, were already working through what she'd seen—and what she'd felt.

There was something about him. It wasn't just the language skills or the Afghan lineage wrapped in an American upbringing. It was the way he carried himself. Controlled. Focused. Careful.

He hadn't smiled once during their conversation, but his eyes had flickered with something—a depth of thought most college seniors didn't possess. And when she'd mentioned Afghanistan, there'd been a shift. Subtle, but telling. Like someone hearing a word that didn't quite belong and trying not to flinch.

Ambar leaned back behind the table bearing the seal of the Central Intelligence Agency. From her vantage point, she could still see him—six-foot-one, trim but solid, the kind of fit that came from discipline,. He moved with deliberate purpose, each step measured, his backpack slung over one shoulder like it had been there his whole life.

"I need more on this kid," Ambar muttered under her breath, opening a discreet note-taking app on her secure tablet beneath the table.

She typed quickly:

Subject: Afsar Ramos
Age: Approx. 21–22
University: Middle Tennessee State – Senior, Int'l Relations
Background: American-born. Afghan maternal heritage.
Languages: Fluent Dari. Conversational Pashto. Near-native Farsi.
Initial Impression: Calm, hyper-rational, guarded.
Gut Check: High potential for HUMINT asset development. Recommend priority flag for deep background and follow-up. Possible field suitability.

She tapped the screen to lock it, then looked up again, eyes narrowing as Afsar finally reached the Army table. He exchanged a few words with the recruiters, nodding as one of them handed him a pamphlet and pointed to a tablet for contact sign-up.

"I don't think you're going to join the Army, kid," Ambar whispered with a faint smile. "I think you're going to work for me."

The sun had already dipped behind the skyline by the time Ambar stepped out of her agency-issued SUV and into the underground parking structure of a nondescript federal building in downtown Nashville. She took the elevator to the fourth floor, where a small satellite office for the Agency's Directorate of Operations maintained a quiet presence under the cover of a government contractor.

Her heels clicked softly on the polished concrete floor as she entered the secure suite. A single light glowed at the reception desk, where her assistant, Ashlynn, was finishing a stack of forms beneath a desk lamp.

"You're late," Ashlynn said with a smirk, not looking up.

"I stopped to ruin a promising young man's predictable future," Ambar replied dryly, shrugging out of her blazer and hanging it on a nearby rack.

Ashlynn raised a brow. "Let me guess—he was headed for a career in finance or law school?"

"Worse. Army officer," Ambar said, walking past the desk toward her glass-walled office.

"Oh, the horror," Ashlynn teased, following her inside with a notepad.

Ambar didn't sit. She paced slowly to the window, her back to Ashlynn, fingers steepled in thought. "His name is Afsar Ramos. Senior at MTSU. International Relations major. Languages—Dari, Pashto, Farsi.”

That made Ashlynn pause. “Afghan heritage?”

“Mother was. She’s deceased. He was raised by his father here in Tennessee.”

Ashlynn was already tapping notes into her secure laptop. “You want me to run the standard background?”

“Yes,” Ambar said, finally turning. “Start with a basic scrape—school records, disciplinary history, academic performance. Then check open-source social media and public records for any red flags. If it’s clean, I’ll authorize the deeper layers.”

Ashlynn gave a short nod. “What’s the goal? Just recruitment, or…?”

Ambar leaned against the edge of her desk, arms crossed. “I don’t know yet. Gut says he’s something special. If his background checks out, I want a psych profile and a full lineage trace.”

“Got it.” Ashlynn turned to go, then stopped. “You think he’s field material?”

“I think he’s the kind of person we’d normally miss,” Ambar said. “And I don’t want to make that mistake.”

Ashlynn finished typing the last few commands into her terminal, watching the system begin its initial scan on Afsar Ramos. The interface flickered with familiar queries—education, public records, and affiliations.

"Alright, the surface-level check's underway," she said, glancing toward Ambar. "I'll let the scrape run overnight and review what comes in first thing."

Ambar nodded, collecting her phone and ID badge from her desk. She reached for her blazer on the hook by the door. "Good. Keep this quiet for now. I don't want his name circulating anywhere outside this room."

Ashlynn smirked. "You mean outside this broom closet masquerading as a federal office?"

Ambar chuckled. "Exactly. No one needs to know we might've found a unicorn today."

Ashlynn leaned back in her chair, stretching her arms. "You heading out?"

"Yeah." Ambar slung her blazer over her shoulder. "Don't stay too late. That database has a tendency to suck you in and keep you prisoner."

Ashlynn waved her off. "I'll be out of here by nine. Maybe."

Ambar gave her a playful look. "Nine, Ash. Not midnight. Go be a human being for a few hours."

"I'll try," Ashlynn replied, already turning back to her monitor.

Ambar stepped out into the dimly lit hallway, the sound of the security door locking behind her with a familiar click. As she walked toward the elevator, her mind returned to Afsar's calm posture, the measured way he spoke, and those eyes that seemed just a little older than his years.

There was something there.

She pressed the elevator button, the floor humming beneath her shoes.

And she intended to find out what it was.

The next morning, Ambar stepped into the office balancing a coffee in one hand and her tablet in the other. The hum of fluorescent lights and the faint buzz of her computer kicking on greeted her like the start of another routine day—except today was anything but routine.

"Morning, boss," Ashlynn called out from her desk, already halfway through her second energy drink. "I left the preliminary results on your desk last night. He's clean—squeaky, actually. GPA's strong, no red flags. You were right. He's… interesting."

Ambar set her coffee down and picked up the folder, flipping it open. "Born in Clarksville. Moved to Water Valley at two. Afghan mother, American father. Languages listed: Farsi, Dari, conversational Pashto…" She trailed off, eyes scanning the highlighted sections of his school records. "No disciplinary issues. Volunteer hours logged. Double minor in Political Science and Linguistics."

"His International Relations professors gave him glowing marks," Ashlynn added, swiveling in her chair. "One of them called him 'a student who thinks like a diplomat and studies like an analyst.' Not bad, huh?"

Ambar looked up, eyes sharp with interest. "Get me a list of his professors. I want to talk to them. Get their office hours if you can."

Ashlynn raised a brow. "You going back to MTSU today?"

"Yeah," Ambar replied, already slipping the folder into her bag. "Something tells me Afsar Ramos is more than just a student with good grades and a clean record. I want to hear what the people who see him every week have to say."

Ashlynn turned back to her screen and started typing. "Copy that. I'll text you the schedule as soon as I have it. You want me to keep the file open while you're gone?"

"Yeah and start digging into his extracurriculars. Clubs, jobs, anything off paper. I want to know how he thinks, not just how he tests."

Ashlynn gave her a mock salute. "You got it. And hey, don't forget to actually eat lunch today. You're not running ops out of Kandahar anymore."

Ambar smirked. "That's what the granola bar in my glovebox is for."

She slung her bag over her shoulder, folder secured inside and headed for the door—her mind already running through possible angles for her conversations with the professors.

Afsar Ramos might not know it yet, but his life was already beginning to change.

The sun hung high over the Middle Tennessee State University campus as students crisscrossed the sidewalks between classes. The breeze carried with it the scent of freshly cut grass and the low hum of student chatter. Ambar blended in well enough in business-casual attire—dark slacks, a pale blouse, and a navy blazer—but her eyes were constantly scanning, evaluating, absorbing.

She had just stepped out of Peck Hall after a brief but enlightening conversation with Dr. Reardon, Afsar's advisor in the Political Science department. Reardon had been quick to sing Afsar's praises.

"Sharp mind," he had said, tapping a pen on his desk. "He doesn't speak to fill the air. When he does speak, everyone listens. I've had grad students who don't think as strategically as that young man. He's got a calm about him… but it's like there's a furnace underneath, always calculating."

Now, with that impression tucked away, Ambar walked toward the student center cafeteria for her next impromptu meeting. She spotted Dr. Janine Caldwell, a linguistics professor, seated at a corner table with a tray of half-eaten salad and her ever-present thermos of tea. Ambar slid into the seat across from her.

"Professor Caldwell?" Ambar asked with a polite smile.

Caldwell looked up, adjusted her glasses, and smiled. "You must be Ms. Shoeston. Reardon told me you might stop by. You've got questions about Afsar?"

"I do. Just trying to get a better sense of him. Reardon said you've had him for a few courses."

"Oh, yes. Two now, and he comes to my office hours like clockwork." Caldwell leaned in slightly. "He's disciplined in a way that's almost… methodical. Not obsessive, mind you, but intentional. And his command of languages—especially Dari and Farsi—is exceptional. I asked once if he'd grown up in Kabul, and he just smiled and said, 'No, just Water Valley.'"

Ambar chuckled lightly, her eyes flicking past Caldwell's shoulder.

Across the cafeteria, seated alone near the window, was Afsar. His posture was relaxed but straight, his tray neatly arranged. He ate in calm, measured bites. A well-worn paperback sat beside his plate—*The Looming Tower.* Students passed him by without notice, though a few paused to exchange quick greetings or short conversations. He smiled, nodded, but didn't rise from his seat. No one lingered long.

Ambar watched him closely, her expression unreadable. There was something in the way he sat, the way his eyes tracked movement—peripheral, instinctive, like someone used to watching their surroundings.

"He keeps to himself?" she asked without taking her eyes off him.

Caldwell followed her gaze and nodded. "Mostly. He's polite. Friendly, even. But he has this… distance. Like he's always half a step removed. Some kids play it off as mystery. With Afsar, I think it's something else. Maybe loss. Or just the weight of having grown up too fast."

Ambar took a sip of her coffee and set the cup down slowly.

"I see," she murmured, still watching Afsar as he returned to his book, tuning out the buzz around him with ease.

The signs were aligning. Language skills. Cultural insight. Academic discipline. Social awareness. Emotional restraint.

All wrapped in a frame that moved like someone who'd been trained to do so, even if unknowingly.

She glanced back at Caldwell. "Thank you, Professor. You've been very helpful."

"Of course," Caldwell said. "He's one of the good ones."

Ambar rose from her seat and gave a final glance at Afsar across the room. He never looked up, never noticed her watching. But she noticed everything.

And the picture was coming together.

Over the next week, Ambar became a ghost on the edges of Afsar's daily life.

She never intervened, never approached him again—not yet—but she was there. Quietly seated in the back of lecture halls, blending in at campus events, standing off to the side in the quad with a coffee cup and dark sunglasses, taking mental notes on his every movement. Each day, Afsar followed his well-worn routine with a precision that only confirmed what she'd already suspected—he was structured, focused, and unobtrusively observant of his surroundings.

He was never late. Never loud. He didn't spend hours glued to his phone like many of his peers. He had a few acquaintances, no real "group." He wasn't reclusive, but he wasn't chasing attention either. He drifted just far enough from the crowd to watch them without being seen.

On Thursday, she spotted him at the library in the mid-afternoon, seated near a window on the second floor. His laptop was open; a few thick books stacked around it. Every so often, he'd glance outside. Watching, thinking.

Ambar jotted something down in her pocket-sized Moleskine: **"Patient. Mind always working. Never disengaged."**

That Friday, she made her most important move yet.

Through a well-placed call and a vague pretense of career development outreach, she arranged a lunch meeting with Jack Ramos, now a local sheriff's deputy and community liaison for veteran services in Water Valley. They met at a modest diner just off the main road, one of those places with squeaky booths, strong coffee, and pictures of the local high school football team on the walls.

Jack was polite but skeptical. His dark eyes, framed by years of weather and grief, studied Ambar carefully as he sipped his sweet tea.

"So," he said slowly, setting his glass down, "you're saying this is a kind of mentorship program for talented students?"

"In a manner of speaking," Ambar replied with a practiced smile. "We keep an eye on promising individuals who may be a good fit for federal service after graduation. Your son stands out."

Jack leaned back slightly, the corner of his mouth twitching in what might've been a faint smile—or a warning.

"Well, I'm not surprised. Afsar's always been that way. Did most of the raising himself after Afsoon passed. Always ahead of the curve. Disciplined to a fault."

"He mentioned her, briefly," Ambar said. "His mother."

Jack nodded. "He's got her strength, no doubt. But also her stubbornness. Doesn't let many people in."

Ambar folded her hands in front of her. "We've noticed that. He seems… self-contained."

"Always has been. After she died, something in him shifted. I think he figured if he stayed on the straightest path possible, he'd never fall apart."

They sat in silence for a beat. Ambar sipped her water. Jack watched her with narrowed eyes.

"You really think he's cut out for federal service?" he asked finally.

"I do," she said without hesitation. "He's got the right instincts. And we need people like him—smart, grounded, culturally fluent, committed to something bigger than themselves."

Jack looked away for a moment, then back at her. "You're not the first person to notice those things about my boy. But I'll tell you this—he won't do anything unless it makes sense to him. He doesn't chase titles. He looks for meaning."

"That's why I'm interested," Ambar said quietly.

Jack nodded slowly, then reached for his wallet to pay for his meal. "Then I guess we'll see what he thinks about all this… when the time comes."

Ambar watched him go, her expression unreadable.

She wasn't trying to force Afsar into anything.

She was simply opening a door.

And waiting to see if he would walk through it.

Two weeks later, the opportunity finally came.

It was a cool, overcast afternoon on campus. Students moved across the quad in scattered clusters—laughing, earbuds in, backpacks slung low. A light breeze stirred the trees, and the hum of campus life buzzed in the background.

Ambar had been on campus for an unrelated meeting with the career services office, but she found herself detouring through the heart of campus, a habit that had become routine these past few weeks.

That's when she saw him.

Afsar sat alone on a stone bench near the fountain, his elbows on his knees, a single sheet of paper held loosely in his hands. He wasn't reading it—just staring at it blankly, eyes dull, shoulders slumped. The usual focus in his posture was gone, replaced by a quiet weight that hung over him like a fog.

Ambar slowed her pace, veering off the sidewalk and circling behind a group of chatting students to get a better angle. From her distance, she couldn't read the letter, but she didn't need to.

The look on his face said enough.

Disappointment. Doubt. The slow sting of a door closing.

She hesitated only for a moment, then made her decision. This was it. The moment she had been waiting for. A crack in his routine, in his guardedness. A window.

Ambar stepped forward, smoothing the front of her coat, her approach quiet but deliberate. As she crossed the open space toward him, the breeze picked up, brushing her hair back, and she thought:

Time to open the door.

And see if he walks through it.

***

2010

The Ramos home sat unusually quiet beneath the soft gray skies of a Tennessee afternoon. Cars lined the gravel shoulder outside the modest, two-story house, and the gentle murmur of voices filtered through the front windows. The scent of freshly brewed coffee, fried chicken, and casseroles filled the air—standard offerings from friends and neighbors doing what little they could.

Inside, the living room was full but subdued. The TV was off. A black-and-white photo of Afsoon sat on the mantle, framed with a single strand of marigolds. The women from church had brought them, Jack's congregation stepping in where they could.

Afsar, eight years old and dressed in a pressed white shirt that tugged slightly at the collar, sat on the edge of the couch, his legs dangling above the floor. His eyes, glassy and unfocused, were locked on the photograph of his mother. He barely blinked.

Jack stood by the kitchen doorway, shaking hands and nodding as people murmured their condolences. He wore his dress blues, the only formal thing he owned, a faint crease in his brow never relaxing. A hand came down on his shoulder—his friend and fellow soldier Sergeant Malloy.

"She was proud of you, Jack," Malloy said quietly. "I could tell. Every time we talked, she was all about you and that boy."

Jack nodded once. "She fought as long as she could." He took a sip of his lukewarm coffee. "I think she held on just to say goodbye."

From the couch, Afsar turned his head slightly as two older women chatted near him in hushed voices.

"Such a beautiful woman," one said, dabbing her eyes with a tissue. "And so young. That heart never was the same after she gave birth, was it?"

"No," the other replied. "She was strong, though. Stronger than most. It's just… the body can only take so much."

The words drifted past Afsar like fog. He looked down at his hands, then over at the empty hallway.

Jack crossed the room and knelt beside his son. "You doin' okay, bud?"

Afsar didn't speak for a moment. Then, softly: "She said I'm meant for something… something bigger. Was that true?"

Jack's throat tightened. He cleared it quietly before speaking.

"She believed it with everything she had, Afsar. And so do I."

He reached out, wrapping an arm around his son's shoulders. "You've got her strength. You'll see."

Afsar nodded, slowly leaning into his father's side.

The front door opened with a soft creak, more people stepping in with solemn expressions and warm dishes in hand. Life, as it always did, continued its quiet crawl forward.

Afsar slid off the edge of the couch, his feet landing soundlessly on the worn hardwood floor. The muffled conversations and the clinking of dishes from the kitchen faded into the background as he wandered toward the far corner of the living room, past a folding table crowded with framed photos and plates of untouched desserts.

He paused by the old bookshelf—his mother's shelf. Her Afghan books, a few worn journals, and a ceramic bowl of prayer beads sat just where she'd left them. On the bottom shelf, half-hidden behind a faded cloth, was a small cedar box. He recognized it immediately. It was his mother's keepsake box. She never let anyone touch it. Not because it was forbidden—just personal. Sacred, in a quiet kind of way.

He knelt and carefully pulled it from the shelf, wiping dust from the carved lid. The floral etchings along the sides had dulled with age, but they were still beautiful. His fingers hesitated on the brass clasp, then gently opened it.

Inside, the scent of sandalwood and rosewater drifted up, soft and familiar. Afsar blinked, holding back tears as he lifted out a folded piece of cloth—a scarf, once vibrant, now dulled with time. Beneath it lay a bundle of old photos, a couple of letters in Farsi, and a smooth stone pendant with a symbol carved into it that he didn't recognize.

"Whatcha got there, Afsar?"

The voice came from behind—his aunt Layla, his father's cousin who'd driven down from Chicago for the funeral.

Afsar turned slightly. "It's Mom's box."

Layla approached slowly, kneeling beside him. Her eyes softened when she saw what he held.

"She used to keep the most important things in there," she said. "Things from home. Things that reminded her of who she was."

Afsar looked down at the scarf, then ran his fingers along the edge of a black-and-white photo—his mother, younger, standing in front of a mud-brick wall with a boy next to her. The boy's eyes looked like hers. He looked like him.

"Who's this?" Afsar asked, holding it up.

Layla's smile faded. She looked at the photo, then back at him. "That's your uncle. Her brother."

"She never talked about him."

"No," Layla said gently. "There were… hard feelings. Stories she didn't want to burden you with. But I'm sure she kept that photo to remind herself of what she left behind."

Afsar nodded and sat back down on the couch, the box still open on his lap. He wasn't sure why, but it felt important to look through it all now, like he was learning something about her—something she couldn't tell him with words.

Jack glanced over from the kitchen doorway, watching his son quietly. He didn't interrupt.

Outside, the clouds began to shift, letting a ray of late-afternoon sun fall through the window and across the box, warming its wooden frame.

Afsar sifted gently through the items, his small hands moving with reverence. Each object told a quiet story—his mother's story. A pair of earrings he had never seen her wear. A postcard from Kabul, the stamp faded. A pressed flower, brittle with time, tucked into a folded piece of notebook paper.

At the bottom, beneath the scarf and the old photographs, he found a single, carefully folded letter. The paper was yellowing at the edges, the creases worn soft. He recognized the script—it was in Dari, the elegant curves and lines that his mother had painstakingly taught him to read over the years, insisting he know her language as well as his own.

He unfolded it with care. The handwriting was precise, beautiful even, though there was a tremble in the ink—like the hand that wrote it had not been steady. He began to read slowly, mouthing the words to himself.

"My dearest daughter Afsoon,
Please come home. We miss you more than words can say. Your father and brother… they have changed. Time has softened them. They understand now the pain they caused and want to make things right. Your father prays for you every night. Your brother asks about you.
You are our light. We are a family, and a family should never stay broken. Come home. Let us heal this.
With all my love,
Your mother."

Afsar stared at the letter, his eyes scanning it again, slower this time, as if trying to feel the words instead of just reading them.

Even at eight, he wasn't naïve. He remembered the long talks between his parents when they thought he wasn't listening. The fearful way his mother avoided certain phone calls. The heaviness in his father's voice when he spoke of "back home." And the scar on his mother's side that she never explained.

He looked at the letter again, this time with quiet skepticism. No matter what promises it made, it didn't feel like the truth. Not the kind his mother had taught him to trust.

He folded the letter back up and placed it gently in the box, between the scarf and the photographs. Then he closed the lid, resting his small hands on the top as if trying to keep the memories from slipping away.

The voices from the kitchen continued in muted tones. Laughter occasionally drifted from the hallway, muted by grief. But Afsar remained still, the cedar box warm on his lap, the smell of rosewater lingering faintly in the air.

He didn't know what kind of man he would become. But in that moment, he knew he would remember. All of it.

Chapter 3

The quad at Middle Tennessee State was unusually quiet for a spring afternoon. A cold breeze rustled the branches above, carrying with it the faint scent of blooming dogwoods and freshly cut grass. Students passed by in lazy strides, their chatter distant and unimportant.

Afsar was sitting alone on one of the long stone benches beneath the shadow of the library, his shoulders hunched and eyes fixed on the piece of paper in his hands. She slowed her pace as she approached, her boots barely crunching the gravel walkway. Her eyes dropped briefly to the document—familiar government-issued font, the unmistakable watermark of the U.S. Army in the upper left-hand corner.

She stopped a few feet away, silent.

Afsar didn't look up right away. He just stared at the letter, as if hoping the words on the page might change with enough focus. Then, sensing her presence, he glanced up, his brows tightening as he recognized her.

"Miss Shoeston," he said flatly, folding the letter in half and pressing it between his fingers. "Didn't expect to see you again."

Ambar gave a soft, practiced smile. "I was walking by. Thought I'd say hello."

"Uh-huh," he said, nodding without much conviction.

She studied him closely—his eyes lacked the usual fire she'd seen during their first conversation. He looked like a man caught between certainty and disappointment, pride and confusion.

"You okay?" she asked, taking a seat beside him without waiting for an invitation.

Afsar let out a small breath through his nose. "Depends on your definition. I got this today." He held up the letter between two fingers.

Ambar tilted her head slightly. "Bad news?"

He looked out across the green lawn, jaw tightening. "It's not bad. It's just… not what I expected." He paused. "Medical disqualification. Minor heart murmur. Nothing serious, they said. But serious enough."

"I'm sorry," Ambar said, and meant it.

Afsar shrugged. "Guess it just sucks when your whole plan falls apart in one envelope."

They sat in silence for a moment, the wind tossing a few fallen petals onto the walkway.

Ambar looked at him from the corner of her eye. "Sometimes a door closes because there's a better one you haven't seen yet."

Afsar smirked faintly. "Sounds like a recruiting slogan."

"Maybe it is," she said with a playful shrug. "But that doesn't make it untrue."

He didn't respond, only nodded slowly, still staring straight ahead.

Ambar leaned forward slightly, elbows resting on her knees. "You said you wanted to serve your country. There's more than one way to do that, Afsar."

He turned to her then, curiosity just beginning to flicker beneath the frustration.

Ambar met his gaze, calm and confident. "Why don't we talk?"

Afsar blinked, unsure if he heard her correctly. "We?"

Ambar nodded slowly, her tone even. "Yes. The Agency. CIA. We're rebuilding—retooling, really—

the Afghanistan directorate. Ever since the military pulled out in 2021, we've had to change the way we operate there."

Afsar looked at her warily. "And what does that mean, exactly?"

She glanced around the quad to make sure no one was lingering too close, then leaned in slightly, her voice lower now. "It means fewer boots on the ground. No uniforms, no convoys. We rely on people who blend in. Who understand the culture. The language. People who can move quietly, observe, gather, report. Sometimes influence."

"And you think I'm one of those people?" Afsar asked, brow raised.

"I think you might be," she said without hesitation. "You've got a unique background. You speak the languages. You've lived your whole life in America, but you still carry the knowledge of a place most people in our business will never understand the way you do."

He sat back on the bench; letter still folded in his hands. "You make it sound like I've already got one foot in."

Ambar smiled lightly. "I wouldn't say that. But you check a lot of boxes. We're being deliberate with who we bring in now. We don't need numbers—we need fit. People who can handle complexity. Ambiguity. People who can think three moves ahead without needing someone to walk them through it."

Afsar was quiet for a beat, his fingers lightly tapping the folded letter against his thigh. "So what, you're here to offer me a job?"

"No," Ambar said. "I'm here to offer you a conversation. If you're interested."

He looked over at her, the edges of curiosity clearly beginning to sharpen. "You said discreet and covert. That sounds a lot like dangerous."

She nodded. "It can be. But you strike me as someone who's not afraid of danger. Just someone who needs to believe it's for something that matters. I've been watching you and looking into your background since we first met."

Afsar's eyes narrowed slightly, and his grip on the letter tightened. "Wait... you've been watching me?"

Ambar didn't flinch. Her expression remained calm and matter-of-fact. "Yes. I have."

He shifted on the bench, incredulous. "You talked to my professors?"

She nodded. "Several. And your academic record. Impressive, by the way. International Relations, top of your class. Analytical writing, conflict theory, language proficiencies… I did my homework."

Afsar sat back again, the wind brushing through the trees overhead. "My dad?" he asked quietly.

Ambar hesitated for just a moment. "Yes. We had lunch last week. I told him I was doing a professional inquiry, which is true. I wanted to get a sense of who you are—not just what's on paper."

His jaw clenched, but he didn't speak.

"I've also watched how you move through the world, Afsar," she continued. "You don't seek out crowds, but you're not isolated. People respect you. When they talk to you, it's always brief—but meaningful. You're deliberate, measured, and aware of your surroundings in a way most people aren't. That's not something I can read on a transcript."

Afsar looked at her, still silent, his mind racing. She could tell he was weighing the intrusion against the intent. Testing her words. Testing her.

"I know that's a lot to hear," she said gently. "But I didn't come here to ambush you. I came because I believe you might have a place in something important—if you're willing to consider it."

Afsar let out a long breath, not angry—just processing. "So, what happens now?"

Ambar offered a small smile. "That depends on you. If you want to learn more about what we are doing and how you can fit into those plans, meet with my boss and myself and let's see what we have for you."

Ambar reached into her leather-bound notebook, tore out a clean sheet of paper, and clicked her pen. She scribbled quickly—a phone number.

"No promises," she said, her voice calm but firm. "No commitments. Just a conversation when you are ready to talk. Feel free to reach out to me when you have any questions or concerns."

Afsar noticed that she had said "when" not "if" like she already knew what his decision was going to be, even though he didn't.

She handed the paper to Afsar, who took it with a mix of hesitation and curiosity, eyes scanning the brief note.

"We'll be expecting your call," she added, rising from the bench. "If you don't reach out, we move on. But I don't think you're the kind of man who ignores doors when they open."

Afsar looked up at her, still quiet, the weight of the Army letter in one hand and this new invitation in the other.

Ambar gave him one last look—measured, sure—and then turned, heels clicking softly on the sidewalk as she walked away across the quad, leaving Afsar sitting alone on the bench, the breeze rustling the papers in his lap and the future suddenly far less certain than it had been just minutes before.

***

2010

Afsar sat frozen on the edge of the couch, his small fingers clutched tightly around the worn letter. The Dari script swam in his eyes as his brain replayed the words again and again—his grandmother's plea, the hollow promises that her father and brother had changed, the insistence that it was safe to come home. Even at eight years old, Afsar knew better. His mother's stories, told only when she felt brave or broken enough to speak them aloud, had painted a darker truth. A truth steeped in shame and fear, and in the quiet terror of what she had fled.

He could still see her face—pale and tired in that hospital bed—but smiling for him, whispering in a fading voice that he was special, that he had a purpose. And now she was gone.

The house buzzed faintly with muffled conversation and clinking dishes, the quiet hum of a wake winding down. Distant family friends stood in clusters, offering support and warmth Afsar couldn't feel. Jack, his father, was still in the kitchen talking to an older woman from church.

The walls suddenly felt too close.

Without a word, Afsar jumped up, the letter still in his hand. His footsteps barely made a sound on the hardwood floor as he darted through the hallway, past the framed photos and the scent of flowers and food. He pushed open the back door and burst into the fading afternoon light.

The frigid air bit at his cheeks, but he didn't stop. He didn't call for anyone. His legs carried him past the garden and down the path behind the house, where the yard met the edge of the woods. Familiar trees loomed ahead, branches bare in the late autumn chill, and still he ran, deeper and deeper into the trees, where no one could see him cry.

The chilly wind whipped at Afsar's jacket as he tore through the underbrush, heart pounding, lungs burning, but he didn't slow down. He didn't stop until he reached the familiar mound tucked into the hillside—a gentle rise choked with vines and fallen leaves, inconspicuous to anyone who didn't know it was there.

Afsar dropped to his knees and crawled through the narrow opening in the hill's side, a passage barely big enough for a child. The inside of the small cave opened into a dark pocket of earth and stone, just tall enough for him to sit upright. Years ago, he had stumbled across it while playing with sticks and pretending to be an explorer. Since then, it had become his sanctuary. A secret place. A safe place.

He curled into himself against the cold dirt floor, the shadows folding around him like a blanket. His fingers still clutched the letter, crumpled now, the script blurred where his tears had smeared the ink.

And then the dam broke.

Afsar sobbed uncontrollably, the grief coming in thick, heaving waves that made his whole body shake. He pressed his forehead to his knees and let it all pour out—anger, confusion, sadness, and the crushing weight of loneliness.

"I miss you," he whispered hoarsely, over and over again. "I miss you, Mama…"

His small voice echoed faintly off the cave's walls, a whisper swallowed by the dark.

Afsar sat in silence as the shadows lengthened outside the cave, the air growing colder with the setting sun. His tears had dried, leaving salty tracks on his cheeks, but the ache inside him felt bottomless. He stared at the dirt floor; arms wrapped tightly around his knees.

Crunch. Crunch.

Footsteps outside.

He stiffened, heart suddenly thumping again—not from fear, but anticipation. He recognized the steady, deliberate pace even before the voice called softly through the narrow opening.

"Afsar?" Jack's voice was low, careful. "You in there, buddy?"

Afsar hesitated, then muttered, "Yeah."

There was a pause, then the rustle of leaves as Jack knelt just outside the entrance. "You okay?"

Afsar swallowed hard. His voice came out small, cracked. "I don't know… I feel like… I feel like I caused all of it. Everything she went through. If she hadn't had me, she could've been happy. She wouldn't have been in pain."

Jack was quiet for a moment. The weight of those words lingered between them. Then his voice came, steady but filled with emotion. "No, son. You were her light, Afsar. You were her joy. Her strength."

Afsar looked toward the cave entrance, eyes wide and glistening.

"She used to tell me," Jack continued, "that no matter what happened—no matter what she'd left behind—you made her whole again. You gave her a reason to keep going, to fight. Everything she went through; she did because she loved you."

The words sank deep into Afsar's chest, warming something inside that had gone cold.

"Come on out," Jack said gently. "Let's go home."

Afsar crawled to the entrance, and Jack reached out a strong hand to help him up. As they stood, father and son, dusk blanketed the woods in deep purples and blues. They didn't say much more, but they didn't need to. The silence between them was full of understanding.

Side by side, they walked through the woods, back toward the house—back toward whatever came next.

Chapter 4

Two weeks had passed since the quiet conversation on the bench in the quad, where Ambar had scribbled a phone number and handed Afsar the kind of opportunity that most people only read about in novels or watch unfold in films. Since then, Afsar hadn't reached out—but neither had he disappeared.

Each day, he carried on his routine, the same steady rhythm that had brought him comfort for years. He attended class, worked out in the campus rec center, and studied at his usual table in the James E. Walker Library near the south-facing windows. But something inside him was shifting.

The late March air had warmed, sweet with the scent of fresh grass and the faint perfume of newly bloomed cherry trees lining the quad. When he walked between classes, a breeze tugged at his sleeves, and the warmth of the sun pressed gently against the back of his neck. Yet, amid all the vibrance of spring, Afsar moved as if a cloud followed him—a thoughtful, inward quiet that his friends picked up on, even if they didn't know why.

"You good, man?" asked his roommate, Devon, as they split a takeout pizza one night, the scent of pepperoni and garlic filling their small apartment. The cheese stretched from the slice in Afsar's hand, snapping as he leaned back on the worn couch.

"Yeah," Afsar answered, chewing slowly. "Just thinking a lot lately."

"About graduation?"

"Something like that," Afsar said, offering a tired smile.

Even the gym, once a sanctuary of muscle memory and predictable effort, now buzzed with distractions. As he gripped the cool, knurled surface of the barbell, the clanging weights around him seemed louder than usual, the echoing thuds of rubber plates against hardwood floor less grounding and more jarring. His workouts were efficient, but the fire was… dimmer.

At night, he'd sit at his desk, the glow of his desk lamp spilling across a spiral notebook filled with pros and cons, scribbled thoughts, and questions he couldn't answer yet. The notebook paper was rough under his fingertips, the ink smudging slightly where his hand dragged across lines written in quiet frustration. He chewed on the end of his pen, the bitter plastic taste lingering as his eyes drifted to the folded scrap of paper tucked under his keyboard—the one Ambar had given him.

The number wasn't for a meeting. Not yet. But it were a placeholder—a door left slightly ajar.

He wasn't sure if he wanted to walk through it.

But he hadn't thrown the paper away, either.

On the fourteenth day, Afsar found himself walking the perimeter of the campus just after dusk. The sky was a swirl of navy and fading amber, the scent of honeysuckle strong near the edge of the university garden. Crickets chirped in the underbrush, and somewhere nearby, someone was playing a saxophone out of a dorm window, the sound lazy, melancholic, and drifting through the cooling air.

Afsar stopped under a lamp post. The yellow light hummed above him, casting a soft glow over the sidewalk. He reached into his pocket and unfolded the worn piece of paper again.

Something deep in his gut told him he couldn't ignore it much longer.

Afsar sat on the edge of his bed, bathed in the soft amber light of early morning that spilled through his window blinds. The room smelled faintly of brewed coffee from the kitchen below, and the air was still and cool against his bare arms. His fingers hovered for a moment over the keypad on the screen of his phone. He paused for a minute before pressing send.

The line rang twice.

"Shoeston," came the familiar voice—sharp, composed, unmistakably focused.

"Good evening, it's Afsar."

There was a brief silence on the other end. Then Ambar's tone softened, and there was the faint sound of her office chair creaking. "Afsar. Good to hear from you. You sound... lighter. Different."

"I guess I am," he replied. "I've been thinking about our last conversation—about everything, really. I'm ready to talk."

Ambar smiled to herself, swirling what remained of her lukewarm coffee in its mug. The office around her buzzed quietly with distant footsteps and the muffled hum of a printer. "I'm glad to hear that. How about we meet somewhere quieter than campus?"

"Sure."

"There's a spot I like—Stones River National Battlefield. Peaceful, open... and you'll get to walk and think at the same time."

Afsar nodded, the memory of past field trips flashing in his mind—wide fields, rows of trees swaying in the breeze, the distinct smell of grass and old stone. "Yeah, I remember it. Sounds good."

"Ten o'clock tomorrow morning. Meet me at the visitor center parking lot. We'll walk and talk."

"I'll be there," Afsar said.

As they hung up, he exhaled and leaned back on the bed. Outside, the wind rustled the spring leaves, and a lawnmower buzzed faintly in the distance. He could still taste the lingering mint of his toothpaste and feel the slight vibration of energy returning to his chest—not nerves but resolve.

And for the first time in weeks, he felt… right.

The sun hung low in the sky as morning broke over Stones River National Battlefield, casting long shadows across the dew-kissed grass. A crisp breeze carried the earthy scent of turned soil and old stone, mingling with the fragrance of wildflowers pushing through the tall grass along the walking trail. The gravel crunched beneath their feet as Afsar and Ambar set off from the visitor center, the winding path curving through fields that had once echoed with cannon fire and shouted commands.

Birdsong filled the air in bursts—warblers and robins greeting the day—punctuated by the distant rumble of a maintenance cart somewhere near the park's outer fence. Afsar wore a gray pullover and jeans; his hands tucked in his pockets. The fresh air felt good on his face, the wind tugging playfully at his hair. He looked over at Ambar, who walked beside him in a tailored jacket, her eyes always scanning—subtle, but practiced.

"Thanks for suggesting this place," Afsar said, breaking the silence. "It's...calming."

Ambar offered a small nod. "I figured it might be. A little history and space to breathe never hurt."

They walked a few more steps before Afsar spoke again, his voice softer now.

"The last couple of weeks... they weren't what I expected. After I got that letter from the Army, I felt like a door just slammed shut in my face. I'd been planning for that path since high school, you know? It made sense to me. Predictable. Disciplined."

He paused, kicking a small stone off the path. It bounced against a weathered memorial marker, the sound sharp in the quiet.

"But something about that moment—sitting there on the bench with that letter in my hand—I realized I wasn't just disappointed. I was...free. Like maybe that door closing was the first real sign I was supposed to look at something else."

Ambar glanced over, her expression unreadable but focused. "So you've been thinking seriously about our conversation?"

"I have," he said. "More than I expected to. I've been trying to pay attention to what matters to me. My mom. What she would have wanted. What I could actually do with what I've been given. My language skills. My understanding of both sides. Her side. My side."

Ambar's shoes crunched softly in the gravel as she kept pace with him. "And what have you come to?"

"I'm still figuring that out," Afsar admitted with a short breath. "But I know I want to be useful. Not just another cog. I want to be... deliberate. Strategic. Not lost in the noise."

Ambar's eyes narrowed just slightly, not in judgment, but in recognition. She felt the shift in him—in the way his shoulders no longer sagged with indecision, in the clarity behind his words. The scent of honeysuckle drifted past on the wind, sweet and subtle.

"That's a good start," she said. "Most people who sit across from us haven't even gotten that far."

They rounded a bend in the trail, and an open clearing revealed a line of cannons pointed toward the tree line, now long rusted but still looming with presence. Afsar slowed his pace, eyeing them thoughtfully.

"Is that what your people are looking for?" he asked. "Someone who knows who they are?"

Ambar looked at him carefully, the rising sun glinting against the surface of her aviators. "That—and someone who understands who they could become."

They paused at the edge of the clearing, where tall grass swayed gently around the old cannon mounts. Afsar inhaled deeply, tasting the faint mineral tang of morning dew still clinging to the leaves, the air rich with the scent of damp earth and stone. A woodpecker knocked methodically in the distance, and a bee buzzed lazily past, dipping into a nearby cluster of wild violets.

Ambar stepped closer, her gaze steady on Afsar. The wind shifted her dark hair slightly, and she adjusted the collar of her coat before speaking.

"We weren't ready," she said quietly, as if the ghosts of the battlefield might overhear her. "When we pulled out of Afghanistan in 2021, the Agency—like the rest of the government—had to come to terms with just how much we misunderstood. Not the terrain. Not the logistics. But the people. The fabric of it all."

Afsar turned toward her, his eyes narrowing slightly. "You're saying you lost touch?"

"I'm saying we never really had it," she replied. "We had assets. Informants. Political allies, sure. But we didn't have enough people who truly *understood* the culture—who could read a room in Kabul like they could in D.C. People who didn't just know the language but could *speak* it with their soul."

Her voice softened, but the words carried weight, dropping between them like stones in still water. Afsar looked down at his feet, one hand grazing a low-hanging branch of pine needles beside the path. The needles scratched against his fingertips—sharp, but grounding.

Ambar continued, her tone measured. "That's why we're rebuilding the directorate from the ground up. This time, it's smaller. Smarter. More precise. Fewer boots, more brains. We don't need dozens of agents throwing cash at tribal leaders. We need five or six people who can sit in a tea house in Herat and *listen*—and be listened to."

Afsar's throat felt dry, and he cleared it before asking, "You think I could be one of those five or six?"

Ambar turned, slowly, to face him fully. Her eyes caught the sunlight just right—bright, unreadable.

"I think you're one of the very few who could speak both to them and for us. That doesn't come from a training manual. It comes from life. From identity."

Afsar blinked, caught between the pride stirring in his chest and the cold prickle of anxiety that followed it. The distant hum of cars beyond the tree line reminded him the world was still turning.

"And what happens," he asked, voice barely above a whisper, "if I say yes?"

She smiled faintly. "Then the real work begins."

Afsar's jaw tightened, and his footsteps slowed along the gravel path. The sun had crept higher now, pressing warmth against their backs, but a chill settled between them. Birds still chirped in the trees, but their song seemed more distant, almost hollow. He paused beside a rusted historical placard half-swallowed by ivy, his eyes fixed on the past but seeing something else entirely.

"I need you to understand something," he said, voice low, but threaded with something darker—controlled fury. "I didn't grow up with some romanticized idea of Afghanistan. I'm not tethered to it by nostalgia or heritage pride."

Ambar turned toward him but said nothing. She heard the shift in his voice—the way the edges had hardened.

"My mother… Afsoon," he continued, the name like a fragile offering, "came here because my father saved her life. Literally. Pulled her into the back of a truck after her brother tried to kill her for running away from her family because of me. Her own father gave the order."

His hand clenched at his side, nails digging into the skin of his palm. The sweet scent of honeysuckle from a nearby thicket now seemed almost mocking.

"She was seventeen. A Teenager and brave enough to defy her family's expectations, their control. And for that, they branded her a traitor to her own blood. She never got over it. Never spoke to them again. Not even after her mother wrote her begging her to come home."

Ambar stayed still, the wind brushing across her face like a whispered apology.

"I found that letter," he went on, eyes narrowing. "After her funeral. I was eight. It was in a box of keepsakes. Written in Dari—she taught me how to read it herself. Her mother promised her that her father and brother had changed. That she'd be safe. Even at that age, I knew it was a lie."

Afsar's voice cracked slightly, and he drew a breath, the air now tasting metallic, like the blood he had once imagined spilled on the streets of Kabul.

"So no," he said sharply, eyes cutting to Ambar. "Don't expect me to carry some banner for a country that tried to murder my mother because she wanted a life of her own. Don't expect me to feel *love* for it. Whatever I am… I'm my father's son. I'm hers. Not theirs."

The leaves rustled gently overhead as silence settled between them again. The solemn stretch of battlefield around them felt almost too fitting—an echo chamber for broken pasts and complicated loyalties.

Ambar finally spoke, her voice low but steady. "I don't want you to love it, Afsar. I want you to understand it. That's what makes you different. That's why you matter."

They stood beneath the skeletal shadow of a sycamore tree, its bark peeling like old skin, revealing pale streaks beneath. The breeze picked up again, rustling through the tall grass, carrying the earthy scent of the nearby creek and the sharpness of freshly cut wood from a trail maintenance crew. Afsar's breath came slowly, evenly, but his eyes stared off toward the tree line, burning with something unresolved.

Ambar took a step closer, her boots crunching softly over scattered pebbles. She let the silence hold for a beat longer, then broke it with measured conviction.

"I can't undo what happened to your mother," she said. Her voice was steady, but not cold—there was weight behind it, earned from experience and intention. "But you have a chance to shape the kind of Afghanistan where girls like her don't have to run. Where boys like you don't have to grow up angry."

Afsar's hands were still clenched at his sides, the leather of his watch strap creaking faintly under the pressure of his fist. A mockingbird let out a long, looping call nearby, drawing no attention from either of them.

"That kind of mission," she continued, "it's personal. And powerful."

Afsar's jaw flexed, and he let out a breath that trembled just slightly at the end. The sun filtered through the canopy now, casting shifting patches of warmth across the path in front of them. He could feel the rising heat from the pavement underfoot, smell the ozone thickening in the air as if a storm might be brewing later. His mouth was dry, the taste of bitterness lingering from a truth he never asked to carry.

He said nothing for a long moment. The wind tugged at the hem of his shirt. A pair of hikers passed behind them, laughing quietly, their footfalls a reminder of the normal world continuing just beyond this crossroad.

Finally, Afsar shifted his weight and looked at her.

"I'm not promising anything," he said, voice low, gravelly with restraint.

Ambar gave a slight nod, accepting it for what it was.

"But I'll meet your boss."

She offered him a faint smile—not triumphant, but respectful.

"Here are the details," she said as she pulled out one of her cards from her pocket and scribbled an address, date, and time on it before handing it over to him.

And with that, the two of them turned slowly, the crunch of gravel underfoot filling the silence as they started the long walk back toward the park entrance.

***

2010

The month that followed Afsoon's funeral unfolded like a heavy fog across the Ramos household. The air inside the modest two-bedroom home in Water Valley was thick with silence, broken only by the occasional creak of old wood, the distant chirp of cicadas, or the clinking of dishes Jack did his best to wash every evening.

Afsar barely spoke. He rose each morning without protest but with hollow eyes. His once bright and curious gaze had dulled into something far away. He moved through his days like a ghost—school, home, dinner, bed. No cartoons. No asking questions. No spontaneous laughter.

Jack noticed, of course. He noticed everything. From the way Afsar pushed food around his plate without eating, to the way he sat in the living room staring at the muted television screen, not watching, just existing. But he didn't press. Not yet.

One Saturday morning, Jack stood at the kitchen sink, the strong smell of Folgers coffee rising from his chipped mug as he watched his son sit motionless on the front porch steps. The boy's small shoulders were hunched, arms wrapped around his knees as he stared into the distance, where the old gravel road disappeared into a curtain of pines.

Jack rubbed the back of his neck, sighing deeply. The morning air was crisp, and the scent of dew-soaked earth drifted in through the screen door.

"He's just grieving," Jack muttered to himself. "Give him space."

Still, he couldn't help but worry.

Later that day, Jack knelt beside the shed out back, rummaging through a toolbox, grease staining his fingers. Afsar had always liked to help him tinker—pass him the wrench, ask what this or that part was for—but today, like every day this past month, the boy had stayed inside. Jack looked up at the window, half-hoping he'd see Afsar's small face watching him, maybe just the flicker of curiosity again.

Nothing.

That night, over dinner, the only sounds were the ticking of the wall clock and the occasional scrape of fork against plate. Jack tried, gently.

"You, uh… You wanna go down to the creek this weekend?" he asked, glancing across the table.

Afsar shook his head without looking up. "No, thanks."

Jack nodded slowly and didn't push further.

After dinner, Afsar sat curled into the arm of the couch, his mother's keepsake box on his lap. He didn't open it—just held it, like a child with a blanket they couldn't part with. His thumb slowly rubbed the edge of the lid.

Jack watched him from the hallway for a few moments before turning away. The wood beneath his boots groaned quietly as he walked down the hall and into his room, closing the door softly behind him.

He wanted to believe this was just grief. That it would pass with time. But deep down, in the part of his heart that always knew when a storm was coming, Jack feared it was something more.

And still, he waited.

Steam curled upward from the plate of spaghetti in front of Afsar, the scent of garlic and marinara sauce mingling with the faint pine of the wood polish Jack had used earlier that afternoon. The clinking of forks against ceramic filled the modest kitchen of the Ramos home, the only other sound aside from the dull hum of the refrigerator and the occasional creak of the old ceiling fan above them. The table was quiet—too quiet.

Jack looked across at his son. The boy had barely touched his food again. His shoulders, once full of restless energy, sat slumped under the weight of something unseen. The spaghetti had gone cold on Afsar's plate, but Jack didn't press him. Not yet.

Afsar poked at a meatball, then finally set his fork down with a quiet clink. "Dad?" he said, his voice hoarse from silence.

Jack looked up immediately. "Yeah, bud?"

Afsar's eyes flickered up to his father's face. "I... I found something. In Mom's box. A letter." He got up from his chair, the wood legs scraping against the tile floor, and walked to his backpack, which hung from a peg by the back door. The rustling of fabric echoed in the kitchen as he retrieved the paper, folded several times and slightly worn at the edges. He returned and carefully laid it on the table like it was something sacred. His small fingers trembled as he unfolded it.

Jack's brow furrowed as he watched.

"It's from someone in her family," Afsar said. "It's in Dari. I could read it—she taught me." His eyes stayed on the words, even as his throat tightened. "They were asking her to come back. Saying they'd changed. That they wouldn't hurt her anymore."

The silence that followed was thick—tangible. The refrigerator clicked off with a sudden stop, making the quiet almost roar in its absence. Jack reached across the table, rough fingers brushing the edge of the letter.

"And?" he asked softly.

Afsar looked up, his dark eyes wet but determined. "Why didn't she go back?"

The weight of the question hovered in the air, heavy and unresolved, like the storm clouds that sometimes rolled in over the hills behind their house. Jack drew in a slow breath, the smells of tomato sauce and warm bread suddenly seeming hollow. He leaned back in his chair, the old wood groaning beneath his frame, his expression darkening as he prepared to answer.

Jack rubbed his hands together slowly, the dry rasp of his calloused palms breaking the silence between them. He let out a deep sigh, one that seemed to come from somewhere far deeper than his lungs.

"Come here, Afsar," he said, his voice low and tired.

Afsar rose and walked around the table. Jack pulled him gently into his lap. The boy smelled like shampoo and the warm dust of a late afternoon spent alone in his room. Jack held him close, steadying his own voice as he began.

"She didn't go back," he said, "because going back would've killed her."

He felt Afsar flinch slightly, but the boy stayed still, listening.

"I met your mom in Afghanistan. I was with a security detail working to secure the countryside. One day, she came running towards us—cut up, bruised, bleeding bad. I thought she was going to die." Jack's voice cracked faintly. "She didn't speak much English, but the pain in her eyes didn't need translating."

He swallowed, and Afsar could feel the heavy rise and fall of his father's chest.

"Her family—her own father and brother—had tried to kill her because she wouldn't marry some old man they chose because she was already pregnant with you. Called it honor. I called it what it was—evil." Jack's voice hardened with the memory. "I got her out of the area. Hid her in safe keeping, then pulled every string I had to get her asylum. And when the papers finally came through, I brought her here."

Afsar looked up at him, the paper still clutched in his hand, now soft and crinkled from his grip. "But the letter… it said they changed."

Jack gave a bitter smile, not cruel, just sad. "They always say that. And maybe they believed it. Maybe they were even sorry. But sorry wasn't going to keep her alive. She knew what kind of world she came from. And she wanted something better for you."

The room was dim now, golden strands of sunlight filtering through the window blinds, casting long shadows across the floor. A cicada droned from outside. Jack stroked Afsar's hair gently.

"She didn't stay away because she stopped loving them. She stayed away because she started loving herself. And you. More than anything."

Afsar sniffed, his nose tingling with the salt of his unshed tears. He nodded slowly, pressing his forehead against his father's shoulder.

"I just miss her," he whispered.

"I know," Jack said. "I do too, every day."

They sat there in silence for a while, wrapped in the smell of warm bread, cold pasta, and the bittersweet ghost of someone they both loved.

Chapter 5

The overcast Monday morning sky blanketed the outskirts of suburban Nashville in a dull gray, the kind that made the world feel just a little quieter, a little more serious. Afsar pulled his jacket tighter as he stepped out of his car and glanced up at the plain, two-story office building before him. The architecture was intentionally unremarkable—muted brick, narrow tinted windows, and a neatly trimmed hedge that wrapped around the front like a ribbon on a dull gift.

He walked across the lot, his boots crunching on the gravel that spilled from the edges of the blacktop. Clutched in his hand was the note Ambar had scribbled on at Stones River—the suite number, 214, underlined twice. Inside, the building smelled faintly of coffee and industrial carpet cleaner, a blend that instantly reminded him of hospitals and DMV lines. He followed the hallway past rows of closed doors, each marked with vague titles like *Consulting* or *Logistics Solutions*, until he came to a plain door marked only with a brushed steel plate: **Suite 214**.

He hesitated for a second, then pushed it open.

The small reception area was warmly lit and modern, decorated in soft earth tones that contrasted with the sterile feel of the hallway. A low hum came from a nearby air vent, blending with the faint, rhythmic tapping of a keyboard. Behind a sleek desk sat a woman who instantly looked up from her monitor with a smile so bright it felt like sunshine cutting through the gray morning.

"Hi there!" she chirped, rising to her feet. "You must be Afsar. I'm Ashlynn."

She was in her mid-twenties, with shoulder-length brown hair that bounced slightly as she moved and hazel eyes that sparkled with easy charm. Her figure was athletic, toned, and confident—not bulky, but built with the kind of grace that suggested years of flipping, flying, and perfect landings. The way she carried herself—shoulders back, chin high—hinted at a past in cheer or gymnastics, maybe both.

Afsar gave a small nod, still absorbing the shift in atmosphere. "Yeah… Afsar Ramos. Nice to meet you."

"Likewise!" she said with that all-American smile, her voice effervescent but professional. "Come on in, have a seat. Ambar just wrapped up a meeting and she's expecting you. Can I get you anything while you wait? Coffee, water, maybe a granola bar?"

He chuckled lightly, the corner of his mouth twitching. "I'm good, thanks."

Ashlynn gestured to a pair of sleek, modern chairs set against the far wall, then walked off down the corridor, her footsteps light and assured.

As Afsar settled into the chair, he let out a slow breath. The cushion beneath him was firmer than expected, the faint whir of a wall-mounted air purifier the only sound now that Ashlynn had gone. He ran his fingers over the textured fabric of the armrest, grounding himself, eyes scanning the room—clean walls, a minimalist landscape print, a discreetly placed security camera in the corner.

The weight of the moment settled on him.

So this is how it begins, he thought.

He glanced toward the hallway, waiting for Ashlynn's return.

Ambar sat behind her desk, finishing an encrypted message on her secure tablet, the soft clicking of digital keys the only sound in the office. A soft knock on the doorframe pulled her attention up.

Ashlynn peeked in, her expression a mix of professionalism and a barely restrained grin. "He's here."

Ambar arched an eyebrow. "Afsar?"

Ashlynn nodded, stepping in with a bit more bounce than usual. "Fifteen minutes early."

Ambar's lips curved in mild surprise. "Punctual. I like that."

Ashlynn leaned casually against the doorframe, arms crossed, the faintest pink tint in her cheeks. "He's also… really cute."

Ambar let out a soft laugh through her nose. "He's young."

"I'm young," Ashlynn shot back with a wink. "Besides, there's something about him—like, brooding but polite. Tall, thoughtful, probably good with dogs and elderly people. Kind of a low-key heartthrob."

Ambar chuckled as she stood, smoothing the front of her navy blazer. "You want me to see if he needs a plus one for his first black site deployment?"

Ashlynn grinned. "You joke, but I'd absolutely pack a go-bag if he asked nicely."

Ambar rolled her eyes, though the smile on her face lingered. "Reel it in, Ash. This one's different."

Ashlynn straightened, nodding more seriously. "Yeah… I can tell."

Ambar walked around her desk and headed for the hallway. Her heels made a steady, deliberate click against the polished floor as she moved. "Let's see if he's ready for the next step."

Back in the reception area, Afsar sat upright, his gaze drifting toward the muted painting on the wall, though his ears perked up at the approaching footsteps.

Afsar heard the approaching women and instinctively stood, straightening his posture. The muted hum of the office gave way to Ambar's presence as she rounded the corner, her composed stride filled with quiet authority. Ashlynn followed just a step behind, still wearing that disarming, dimpled smile that had greeted him when he arrived.

Ambar extended a hand. "Mr. Ramos," she said, her voice smooth and professional, "you have no idea how refreshing it is to have someone who shows up fifteen minutes early."

Afsar shook her hand, his grip firm but respectful, a flicker of amusement in his dark eyes. "It's the Baptist in me," he replied with a small grin. "We're very forgiving people… except when it comes to time."

Ambar let out a soft laugh, one that reached her eyes. "I'll keep that in mind."

She turned to lead him down the hall, her pace confident but unhurried. As Afsar followed, he glanced back toward the reception area and caught Ashlynn's eye. With a flicker of a grin and a coy lift of one eyebrow, he gave her a brief smile—equal parts charm and curiosity.

Ashlynn, caught mid-sip of her iced coffee, nearly missed her mouth. She quickly composed herself with a grin of her own and mouthed a subtle, amused "oh my God" as he disappeared down the hallway.

Ambar, without looking back, spoke lightly over her shoulder. "Careful with that smile, Afsar. We're still evaluating your threat level."

Afsar chuckled. "I promise it's only dangerous in close proximity."

Ambar smirked but didn't reply, pushing open a door to a quieter section of the office. The conversation—and the opportunity—was about to begin in earnest.

Ambar's office was minimalist but not cold—clean lines, warm wood finishes, and a window that let in just enough morning sun to soften the edges of the room. Afsar sat across from her in a plush chair, legs crossed at the ankle, his hands resting loosely in his lap. The faint scent of her citrusy perfume mingled with the sharper note of brewed coffee from the corner of the room.

"So…" Ambar leaned back, the leather of her chair creaking lightly. "Did you manage to dodge Ashlynn's charm offensive out there?"

Afsar grinned. "Barely. She's… persistent. But friendly. Definitely a tactical advantage for you."

"She's a professional," Ambar replied with mock seriousness, then cracked a smile. "Also, she's been trying to guess your background for days."

"Oh really?" Afsar raised an eyebrow. "What's the leading theory?"

"Half-Tajik, half-actor from a CW drama."

Afsar laughed, a quiet and genuine sound. "Tell her I'm flattered."

They chatted casually, about Nashville traffic, the unseasonably cool spring morning, and the old school field trip Ambar once took to Stones River. The conversation had just shifted to food—Ambar lamenting the lack of good Kabuli palaw in the city—when the door clicked open behind her.

"Apologies," came a gravelly voice. "I got wrapped up in a briefing."

Ambar stood, smoothing the hem of her blazer. "Robert. You're just in time."

Afsar rose to his feet, his posture composed and attentive. The man in the doorway was as Ambar had described—mid-fifties, face carved with long hours and political fatigue. His salt-and-pepper hair was combed with minimal effort, and his slate gray suit bore the slight rumple of someone who'd been in it since before sunrise.

"Mr. Ramos," Afsar said, extending his hand with a firm, respectful grip. "Thank you for making time today."

Robert returned the handshake, eyeing the young man with an unreadable expression. "It's just Robert here. Let's skip the formalities. You're the one we've been hearing about."

He gave Ambar a glance, then motioned to the chair. "Let's sit. I want to get a read on you."

Afsar nodded, the faint scent of old paper and coffee intensifying as Robert took his seat across from him, flipping open a worn leather folio. The room quieted as the conversation turned to matters far more serious.

Robert leaned back in his chair, steepling his fingers over his folio. His gaze settled firmly on Afsar. "Let's start at the beginning. Tell me about your family."

Afsar nodded slowly, sitting upright, his palms resting on his thighs. "My father's American—Southern, blue-collar roots. My mother was Afghan. She came to the U.S. before I was born."

Robert didn't write anything yet. "You close with them?"

"My father and I are close, yes. Always have been. My mother passed away when I was eight."

"I'm sorry to hear that," Robert said, his tone genuine. "Was her passing… sudden?"

Afsar looked past them for a moment, gathering his words. "Congestive heart failure. Sudden enough for me. She was young."

Robert nodded once, jotting a brief note. "And how did that affect you growing up?"

Afsar gave a half-smile with no humor in it. "It made me quiet for a long time. I withdrew. Tried to make sense of it on my own."

"Still trying?" Robert asked, not unkindly.

"Maybe," Afsar replied after a pause. "Maybe I'm just better at hiding it now."

Robert shifted gears. "What are you studying?"

"International relations and political science," Afsar answered. "Minoring in Middle Eastern studies."

"Why?"

"Because I grew up between two worlds. Because I want to understand the fault lines that crack people apart. And maybe learn how to exploit them for my purposes."

Robert raised a brow at that but didn't comment. "Languages?"

"English, Dari, Pashto. Some Arabic—enough to get by, not enough to impress a cleric. Spanish from high school, but don't test me. I am also very fluent in Farsi."

Robert cracked a faint smile. "I won't. What do you do when you're not reading about geopolitics?"

Afsar chuckled softly. "I run. I box at a local gym. I read—mostly history and fiction. I volunteer sometimes with a refugee resettlement group. I like to cook, mostly my mother's recipes."

"Any friends you're particularly close to?" Robert asked.

"A few," Afsar said. "But I keep a small circle. I'm not exactly the life of the party."

Robert nodded slowly, jotting again. "And what do you hate?"

Afsar met his gaze. "Cruelty. Hypocrisy. Bureaucracy for the sake of itself. People who hurt others just because they can."

Robert looked at him a beat longer before moving on. "What cultures have shaped you the most?"

Afsar exhaled. "American and Afghan, obviously. But also the military one, through my dad. Discipline, service, all that. And I've learned a lot from the immigrant community in general—how to survive, adapt, and stay rooted."

Robert closed his folio. "You're a hybrid. That's a rare asset."

"I'm also a risk," Afsar said, voice even.

Robert didn't deny it. "Most people are."

There was a beat of silence before Robert stood. "That's all I need for now."

Ambar stood as well. "You did great," she said, her voice warm.

"Thanks," Afsar replied, though there was a quiet weight in his eyes.

The three walked together down the hallway, their footsteps muffled against the carpeted floor. The scent of coffee and toner lingered faintly in the air. As they reached the reception area, Ashlynn glanced up from her desk, offering Afsar a hopeful smile that he returned with a polite nod.

"Thank you both," Afsar said, turning to Robert and Ambar.

Robert offered a firm handshake. "We'll be in touch soon."

Ambar gave him a softer handshake and a knowing look. "Take care of yourself, Afsar."

Before Afsar made it out of the building, he turned around and headed back to the office. Once he returned, he made sure no one else was around except for Ashlynn and said, "I think your area cute and nice and I would like to get to know you better over coffee or dinner." He grabbed a sticky notepad off her desk and scribbled his name and number on the top page. "Call me sometime and let's set something up." She followed his lead and did the same with her number on the next note and handed it to him as he started to leave.

Robert stood by the window in Ambar's office, arms crossed as he watched Afsar walk across the parking lot below, his stride steady, purposeful, but with just enough tension in the shoulders to reveal a weight still hanging on him. The older man's brows were furrowed in thought, a silence stretching between them.

Ambar sat behind her desk, waiting him out.

Finally, Robert exhaled. "He's sharp. Polished in a rough-cut kind of way. But…" He turned from the window to face her. "There's something off. Like a wire pulled too tight. I don't know if it'll hold or snap."

Ambar didn't flinch. "He's been through a lot. Most people have wires—his just aren't hidden behind a resume or a government badge."

Robert raised an eyebrow. "You don't think the personal baggage will get in the way?"

"I think the personal baggage is the point," Ambar replied firmly. "That's the kind of edge we *need* in the Directorate. He understands the stakes—not in theory, but in his bones."

Robert folded his arms again; lips pressed into a tight line. "You've been grooming him from the beginning."

"I've been watching him," she corrected. "He's not perfect, but he's *right*. He's got language, cultural fluency, emotional intelligence, a mind sharp enough to cut glass—and he's looking for a purpose."

Robert let that settle in the air for a moment, pacing once behind the chair. "He's angry."

"He's focused," Ambar countered. "That anger is directed, not destructive. He wants to *build* something better—even if he doesn't admit it yet."

Robert stopped, watching her. "Your gut, huh?"

"Every time," she said with a confident smile. "And you know I don't bet light."

He grunted, then sighed, shaking his head with a reluctant smirk. "Push him through to the next phase. But keep a close eye."

"I already am."

Robert reached for the door, pausing as he looked back at her. "If he blows up in our face, it's on you."

"I'll take that risk," Ambar said, her eyes steady. "Because if he doesn't… he might just be the best asset we've had in years."

Robert gave a quiet nod and disappeared down the hallway, leaving Ambar alone with the hum of the overhead lights and the echo of potential rising in her chest.

∗∗∗

2014

The chill of the Tennessee morning clung to the pine-needled ground like a secret. A pale orange glow bled through the trees as the sun pushed its way up over the horizon. Smoke curled from the stovepipe chimney of the family's old deer camp cabin—half cedar, half rusted tin—nestled between two gentle hills deep in the woods of Wayne County.

Inside, the scent of fried bacon and fresh coffee filled the small cabin, mingling with the earthy musk of gun oil and damp camouflage hanging by the door. Boots were lined up in varying sizes, and a couple of rifles leaned against the wall with the reverence of sacred instruments.

Twelve-year-old Afsar was a whirlwind of motion, bouncing on the balls of his feet like a boxer before the first bell. He was already dressed—camo from head to toe, bright-eyed, and buzzing with anticipation. The oversized jacket nearly swallowed him, and the blaze orange vest he wore seemed to float like a safety flag on a ball of energy.

"Dad! Dad! You said we'd leave at first light! That's *now*! Let's go!" Afsar burst into the kitchen where his father, Jack, was pouring himself a mug of coffee, moving with the slow, deliberate calm of a man who'd been doing this for decades.

Jack looked over the rim of the mug at his son, lips curling into a grin. "Son, the deer ain't goin' anywhere. If you scare everything within a ten-mile radius before we even leave the cabin, we're liable to spend the whole morning watchin' squirrels."

"I'll be quiet in the woods, I promise," Afsar said, lowering his voice suddenly to a whisper and pantomiming tiptoeing, his fingers in front of his mouth like a cartoon spy. "See? Stealth mode activated."

Jack chuckled and reached for the thermos. "Get your boots on and check your pack one more time. You got your handwarmers? Extra shells?"

"Yes, yes, and yes," Afsar rattled off, zipping open his daypack for the third time that morning and proudly displaying the contents. "Water, jerky, binoculars, gloves, flashlight, emergency whistle, compass, and...a Snickers bar. You said I'd need energy."

"You listen better than half the grown men I take out here," Jack said, walking over and giving his son a firm pat on the shoulder. "You nervous?"

Afsar hesitated for a heartbeat, his excitement dimming just a notch. "A little. What if I mess it up? What if I freeze or miss or…"

"Then you miss," Jack said simply. "And we learn from it. Nobody hits a buck their first time. You're not out here just to shoot—you're out here to *hunt*. To listen. To learn. To respect what's around you. The woods'll teach you if you're quiet enough to hear it."

Afsar nodded, the seriousness of his father's words grounding him a bit. He tugged his gloves snug, then grabbed his .243 rifle from the wall rack—his birthday present from Jack just a few months back, cleaned and checked three times since yesterday.

"I'm ready, Dad."

Jack smiled again and opened the cabin door. A gust of crisp, pine-scented air swept in, brushing across their faces and carrying the distant caw of a crow. The forest beyond beckoned—ancient, watchful, and waiting.

"Well then," Jack said, stepping onto the frosted steps. "Let's go make a memory."

Afsar followed eagerly, boots crunching against the frozen leaves as the two disappeared into the woods.

Afsar had just stepped off the porch behind his father when he heard the familiar *putter-chuff* of an old engine idling. The soft sound of gravel crunching under tires turned his head.

Around the side of the cabin came the family's camo-wrapped side-by-side utility vehicle, driven by none other than his grandfather, Hank Ramos—straw

Stetson low on his brow, gray beard full and wind-swept, and his ever-present toothpick shifting from one side of his mouth to the other.

"There's my huntin' partner!" Hank called out, voice raspy with age but lit with pride as he brought the vehicle to a stop beside them. "You ready to get your boots muddy, Ace?"

Afsar grinned and jogged over. "Yes, sir! I'm *so* ready."

Hank chuckled as he stepped down from the side-by-side. "Well then, let's get this show on the road."

They made quick work of stashing their gear in the back—rifles in padded cases, packs, a small cooler with sandwiches, and a thermos of hot cocoa that Hank had packed "just in case the boy gets cold." The metallic clink of the tailgate shutting echoed through the trees, the scent of pine and damp leaves thick in the cold morning air.

Jack wiped his hands on his jeans and looked at Afsar seriously, his tone shifting. "Alright, son. Before we get out there, it's time for the talk. Huntin' ain't just about aim and fire. There are rules—unwritten ones and plain old common sense."

Hank leaned against the front bumper, arms crossed. "First off, safety. That rifle doesn't come off safety unless you're lookin' through the scope at a clear target. You don't shoot at movement. You don't shoot at sound. You *see* the animal, clear and still, and you know what's beyond it before you so much as breathe on the trigger. Got it?"

"Yes, sir," Afsar said, standing straighter.

Jack nodded. "Second, patience. The woods aren't a video game. Sometimes we sit for hours and don't see a thing. That's part of the hunt. You learn to *listen*— to the birds, the wind, the stillness. The woods'll tell you what's around, but only if you stop runnin' your mouth."

"I'll be quiet," Afsar promised, his voice hushed now, eyes darting from his father to his grandfather, taking it all in.

"Third," Hank said, his voice softer now. "Respect. You don't pull that trigger unless you're sure. Not just because of safety, but because takin' a life—any life— is serious business. You make it clean. You make it count. You take care of what you kill."

Afsar nodded solemnly, the weight of their words pressing into his young chest. "I understand."

Hank gave him a satisfied nod and clapped a calloused hand on his shoulder. "You're gonna do fine, Ace. I see your mama's heart and your daddy's spine in you. You just remember that out there."

Afsar felt his cheeks flush—not from the cold, but from pride swelling in his chest. He looked up at the two men he admired more than anyone, both seasoned and steady, forged by life and land.

"Let's go find some deer," he said quietly, sliding onto the back bench of the side-by-side.

The engine growled as Hank fired it back up, the scent of gasoline and morning air blending in Afsar's nose as they rolled off into the woods, tires chewing softly through leaves and damp earth, the hunt just beginning.

The chill in the blind had set deep into Afsar's bones. Three hours of waiting, whispering, and watching had left his eyes tired and his hands cold despite the gloves. Hank and Jack sat on either side of him in the narrow wooden box, thermoses empty and silence long settled in.

Jack glanced at his watch and sighed. "Alright, boys… I reckon we give it ten more minutes, then pack it in."

Afsar was just beginning to shift his weight when Hank's whisper cut through the quiet like a knife.

"Hold up… right there… tree line at one o'clock."

Afsar froze, eyes darting where his grandfather pointed. Emerging cautiously from the edge of the woods was a huge, broad-shouldered ten-point buck, its antlers catching the pale light like twisted branches of polished bone. It stepped carefully into the clearing, pausing to sniff the air, its breath rising in little clouds.

"Big fella," Hank muttered, barely audible. "That's a prize."

Jack reached slowly for the rifle leaning against the wall beside Afsar. "Alright, son," he whispered, pressing it into Afsar's gloved hands. "You've got this. Breathe slow. Take your time. Center mass, just behind the shoulder."

Afsar nodded, his heart thudding hard enough to feel in his throat. He rested the rifle on the padded ledge of the blind, peering through the scope. The crosshairs danced for a moment as his breath fought him.

"Steady," Jack murmured. "Just like we practiced. Let your breath settle. Let your body settle."

Hank leaned in close to Afsar's ear. His voice was low and sharp, like flint striking steel. "Imagine that deer is someone you hate. Not just dislike—*hate*. And this is your one shot to do something about it."

Afsar didn't respond. His fingers tightened slightly. The cold faded. The forest fell away. In the tunnel of the scope, the buck stood perfectly still, broad chest exposed, looking off toward the distant trees.

*Click—*safety off.

He took a breath. Then another.

Crack.

The rifle kicked against his shoulder, and the sharp scent of gunpowder mixed with pine sap and dried leaves. The sound echoed through the trees and died out in the hush that followed. The buck leapt once— and collapsed, legs folding beneath it.

The blind erupted in hushed celebration.

"Well I'll be damned," Hank said, slapping his knee. "That was clean. Dropped him like a sack of rocks."

Jack clapped Afsar on the back, pride in his eyes. "That's how it's done, son."

By the time they reached the downed buck and secured it to the back of the side-by-side, the adrenaline had turned to quiet awe. The men worked together in practiced rhythm, ropes tightened and antlers wrapped in canvas.

The vehicle bumped and jostled as they made their way back toward camp, the sun dipping lower in the sky and the smell of fresh earth and blood filling the frigid air.

Jack looked back at his son, who was sitting next to the buck, staring at it in silence.

"You did good today, Afsar," he said. "I gotta ask… when you pulled that trigger, what were you thinkin' about?"

Afsar looked up, face still and unreadable, but his voice was as clear as the gunshot had been.

"My mother's father."

Chapter 6

The sky was still overcast when Afsar pulled into a cracked, gravel-dusted parking lot tucked deep in Nashville's aging Warehouse District. Old brick buildings with faded signage loomed around him, the sort of place people passed without ever noticing. The building he'd been instructed to find—Suite 4B—had no name on the door, just a plain metal number screwed into flaking beige paint.

He stepped out of his car and zipped his black jacket up to his chin against the early morning chill. The smell of damp asphalt and rust lingered in the air. Afsar paused for a moment, eyes scanning the building's exterior—no windows on the lower level, a single security camera over the doorway, a keypad entry system.

Looks like nothing, he thought. *Which means it's probably everything.*

He entered the front door, the faint hum of fluorescent lights and the sterile tang of disinfectant immediately hitting his nose. The lobby was minimalist and unadorned—gray walls, clean tile floors, and a receptionist's desk made of brushed aluminum and white laminate. Behind the desk sat a middle-aged man in navy scrubs, reading a clipboard.

The man looked up, offered a polite but neutral nod. "Can I help you?"

Afsar stepped forward. "I'm here for… evaluation. Name's Afsar Ramos."

The man checked his clipboard, then tapped a button under the desk. A lock buzzed on the door to the left. "Follow the green line on the floor. Someone will meet you at Station 3."

Afsar looked down—three colored lines, green, blue, and red, stretched from the lobby like the Yellow Brick Road, winding through the corridor ahead. He followed the green one, his footsteps soft against the linoleum. Along the hall, he passed doors with small, frosted-glass windows and metal plates reading things like "Trauma Simulation Room" and "Emergency Field Medicine Lab."

As he moved farther in, the faint sound of muffled voices echoed behind closed doors. A crash of a metal tray, a sharp command shouted in urgency—it wasn't a hospital, but it wasn't play-acting either.

At Station 3, a woman in her forties with short-cropped blond hair and a clipboard was waiting for him. She wore olive drab cargo pants and a charcoal-gray T-shirt that read **MEDOPS** in faded block letters. Her eyes were sharp, assessing.

"Afsar Ramos?" she asked, extending a hand.

"Yes, ma'am."

"I'm Harper. I'll be coordinating your assessment today." She gave him a nod of approval. "You're early. That's a good habit. Come with me. Let's see what you're made of."

As she turned and led him deeper into the facility, the hum of equipment grew louder, mixing with the beeping of heart monitors and the antiseptic chill that seemed to settle in the bones. The sharp scent of alcohol wipes hit his nose as they passed a room where two techs were resetting a CPR dummy.

Afsar's hands flexed at his sides, nerves and adrenaline surging.

Whatever this place is, he thought, *it's not just about medicine.*

Harper led Afsar down a narrow corridor, her boots echoing on the tile floor in a steady rhythm. The hallway smelled of latex and something sterile, like cold steel and antiseptic—clean, but impersonal. Afsar followed close behind, absorbing every detail: the emergency supply lockers lining the wall, the distant mechanical *whirr* of a defibrillator being tested, and the clipped voices of personnel behind closed doors.

They stopped at a plain door labeled **Exam Room 6**. Harper pushed it open and motioned him inside.

The room was utilitarian—bright overhead lighting, a paper-lined exam table, a stainless steel sink, and a cabinet stocked with medical instruments. A monitor hummed softly in the corner, displaying vital sign readings from a previous use. It smelled of iodine and plastic.

"Take a seat on the table," Harper said, flipping open her clipboard. "This part's pretty straightforward. Height, weight, blood pressure, reflexes, the usual. Shirt off, please."

Afsar complied, tugging his black hoodie over his head and folding it neatly beside him. The freezing air prickled against his skin, raising goosebumps along his arms. Harper gave him a quick once-over, clinical but efficient.

"You work out?" she asked, wrapping the blood pressure cuff around his arm.

"Not as much as I should. Just runs and bodyweight stuff mostly."

She nodded, pumping the cuff. "Well, you've got a runner's heart. Resting pulse is good." She scribbled a note. "Lift your arms—yeah, just like that. Any joint pain? Old injuries?"

"No, ma'am."

She ran through the rest of the exam briskly—checking reflexes with a rubber hammer, listening to his lungs and heart with a cold stethoscope, tapping his knees and wrists with practiced rhythm.

"Breathe in… hold it… and out." Her tone was clipped but calm. "Again."

Afsar followed instructions, the cold stethoscope pressing into his back like ice. He inhaled deeply, catching the faint tang of rubbing alcohol and latex gloves.

"Everything sounds clear," she said, pulling back. "Blood draw's next, then a basic vision and hearing check."

As she swabbed the inside of his elbow, Afsar turned his head away. "So, this is all just… medical?"

"For now," Harper replied as she inserted the needle with the efficiency of someone who'd done it a thousand times. "We need to know the machine works before we ask it to run hard."

Afsar let out a soft exhale, watching the crimson line fill the tube.

"What comes after this?" he asked, his voice low.

Harper gave a faint smile as she capped the vial and labeled it. "After this? We test your mind. And your instincts."

She placed the vial in a tray and looked him in the eye. "But let's finish checking the body first."

There was a knock—two short raps—on the exam room door. Harper glanced toward it just as it creaked open. A tall, broad-shouldered man in scrubs stepped in. His head was shaved clean, and he wore a closely cropped beard. His name tag read **D. Maclin, R.N.**, and a warm, professional smile broke across his face as he stepped into the room.

"Morning," he said, voice smooth and deep. "Afsar Ramos?"

Afsar, still seated on the edge of the exam table, nodded. "Yeah, that's me."

Maclin extended a hand. "I'm Darius. I'll be guiding you through the rest of today's eval. Harper, we good on vitals?"

"Vitals are clean," Harper replied, peeling off her gloves and dropping them into the waste bin. "No red flags. He's all yours."

"Appreciate it." Darius turned back to Afsar. "You can grab your hoodie but leave the shoes off for now. We've got a walk to another suite."

As Afsar pulled on his hoodie and followed Darius into the hallway, he noticed a subtle change in atmosphere. The halls here were quieter, less clinical. The fluorescent lighting gave way to softer LEDs overhead, and the air carried a different smell—something sterile, yes, but mixed with leather and a faint metallic tang that felt… heavier.

"So, uh… what exactly is the next part?" Afsar asked, his voice steady but cautious.

Darius offered a sympathetic smile. "It's a bit more in-depth than the standard physical. We're looking at your resilience—biometric scans, endurance thresholds, and even some mild stress tests. The doc checked the hardware. Now we look at the wiring."

Afsar gave a faint chuckle. "Sounds intense."

Darius glanced at him sideways. "That's because it is."

They reached an unmarked steel door with a keypad. Darius tapped in a code and opened it, revealing a new space: a brightly lit exam suite outfitted more like a testing lab. A central exam chair sat in the middle, flanked by monitors, machines, and a rolling tray lined with sealed instrument packs. A faint mechanical hum filled the air, and the temperature dropped a couple degrees. It smelled of ozone, alcohol, and something faintly metallic.

"Take a seat," Darius said, gesturing to the chair. "We're going to run through everything—EKG, EEG, core temp and sweat response, a couple scans. Then we move on to the more… nuanced stuff."

Afsar sat, settling into the cold vinyl cushion, which conformed slightly to his weight. "Define nuanced?"

Darius chuckled, picking up a clipboard. "Let's just say we'll see how your body responds to pressure. Controlled, of course. Just enough to understand your baseline."

He began attaching sensors to Afsar's temples and chest. The adhesive pads were cool against his skin.

"You nervous?" Darius asked, not looking up.

Afsar exhaled through his nose. "Only about not knowing what comes next."

"Fair answer," Darius said, connecting the final lead. "But that's part of the test too."

He flicked a switch, and a low beep echoed through the room. The screens flickered to life, displaying pulsing lines and biometric data in real time. Afsar's heartbeat pulsed steadily, a rhythmic *beep… beep… beep* filling the silence.

Darius stood back, arms folded. "Alright, Afsar. Let's see what you're made of."

Darius moved with the quiet efficiency of someone who had done this a thousand times. He tapped a few keys on the workstation and studied the first set of readouts.

"Heart rate's steady. Breathing's smooth. No red line reactions. That's a good start," he said, his eyes still on the screen. "Now I'm going to dim the lights and run a few sensory-response tests. Keep your eyes open and focus straight ahead."

The lights above dimmed to a soft bluish hue. Afsar blinked, his pupils adjusting quickly. He could hear the soft *whir* of the machines and the faint hiss of the air vent overhead. His skin prickled as the cooler temperature of the room seeped into his arms through the fabric of his hoodie.

Darius moved in front of him with a small penlight.

"I'm going to run this across your field of vision. Just follow it with your eyes—don't move your head."

Afsar nodded, watching as the light moved in slow arcs. His eyes tracked it dutifully.

"Good. Now close your eyes. I'm going to touch various points on your body. Just tell me when you feel something."

Afsar shut his eyes. The room fell quiet. Then—a tap on his left forearm.

"Now."

"Good. Next."

Another tap, this time on his shin. "Now."

The tests continued—pressure on his shoulders, brush against his fingers, the cool press of a gloved hand to the back of his neck.

"Alright, open up," Darius said.

Afsar opened his eyes to the brighter overhead lights flickering back on.

"Now for thermal," Darius said. He wheeled over a sleek, metallic device with a retractable wand. "I'm going to apply both cold and heat to your skin. Just give me a one-to-ten rating based on discomfort. Ten being *absolutely unbearable*."

He pressed the wand to Afsar's inner wrist. It was ice-cold, like winter steel. Afsar flinched slightly.

"Four," he said.

"Nice," Darius murmured. He pressed a few buttons, and the wand warmed rapidly—now hot, but not scalding.

"Six," Afsar replied with a wince.

"Alright, resilience intact. Next up, resistance thresholds."

Darius rolled a cart over with a stress grip sensor and a heart monitor strap.

"Place your hand here. Squeeze when I tell you to. We'll measure the strength and endurance of your grip under timed pressure."

Afsar did as instructed, wrapping his hand around the cold plastic handle.

"Now. Squeeze and hold."

The grip tensed under his fingers. Beads of sweat formed at his temple as he fought to maintain the pressure.

"Still holding… good. You're into the endurance zone now…"

Afsar's jaw clenched. His biceps trembled slightly under his sleeve.

"And release."

Afsar exhaled sharply and shook out his hand.

"Damn," he muttered, flexing his fingers.

Darius grinned. "You've got more in the tank than you thought."

He checked the display, nodding with satisfaction. "Impressive numbers. One last section before we wrap this phase—biofeedback. We're going to measure how you respond to an adrenaline spike."

"How do you plan to spike my adrenaline?" Afsar asked warily.

Darius's grin widened just enough to be mischievous.

"Nothing extreme. Controlled simulation, vivid audio and imagery. Think of it like your body being dropped into the middle of chaos… without the actual danger."

Afsar sat back against the chair and smirked faintly. "Alright. Let's see what kind of chaos you've got."

Darius stepped over to a panel on the wall, dimming the lights again and starting the next sequence.

"Hang tight," he said. "We're about to kick things up a notch."

The lights brightened as the simulation ended, the mechanical hum of the equipment winding down with a soft click. Afsar exhaled slowly, flexing his fingers as the tension left his body.

Darius removed the heart monitor strap and patted Afsar's shoulder. "You did well. Numbers are strong, better than most we get in here."

"Glad to hear it," Afsar said, rolling his neck to work out a kink.

"Come on," Darius said, gesturing toward the door. "There's one more stop on the tour."

They exited the sterile exam room and stepped into a different hallway—this one subtly warmer, the lighting softer and more natural. The walls were painted in warm earth tones and adorned with framed black-and-white photographs of vintage medical teams and historic field units. There was the faint scent of cedar and leather in the air, a far cry from the antiseptic tang of the exam room.

Darius led Afsar to a tall oak door with a brass nameplate that read simply: **Room 3B**.

"This is your last stop for today," Darius said. "No wires, no needles—just a conversation. You'll be fine."

He opened the door and gestured Afsar inside.

The room beyond was nothing like the rest of the building. Afsar stepped into a space that felt more like his dad's study at home than a government facility. The walls were lined with bookshelves that bowed slightly under the weight of their contents—leather-bound volumes, dog-eared paperbacks, and thick academic tomes. A deep burgundy Persian rug stretched across the hardwood floor, anchoring a set of polished leather chairs and a matching couch. A side table held a tea service, the subtle aroma of bergamot rising from the steam curling up from a porcelain cup.

Afsar stepped further in and ran a hand along the smooth leather arm of the couch before settling down, the cushions creaking slightly beneath him. The warmth of the room wrapped around him like a blanket, and for the first time that day, his shoulders relaxed.

He barely had time to fully take it in when the door opened again behind him.

A middle-aged man entered—tall, broad-shouldered, dressed in a charcoal gray pullover and slacks. His hair was black streaked with silver at the temples, and he moved with the quiet, deliberate confidence of someone used to watching without being seen.

"Mr. Ramos," the man said, his voice calm and even. "I'm Dr. Porter."

Afsar stood, extending a hand. "Nice to meet you, sir."

Dr. Porter shook it with a firm, measured grip. "You've had a long morning. You holding up alright?"

"I've had worse," Afsar said with a faint smile as he returned to his seat.

Porter nodded approvingly and took the armchair opposite him. "Good. Let's talk, then."

Dr. Porter leaned back in the leather armchair, resting one ankle casually over his knee. He studied Afsar for a moment—not intrusively, but like a craftsman taking the measure of a tool before putting it to use.

"The physical checks out," he said, his voice low and smooth. "But the mind is where most of the work is done in this line of work. And where most of the danger lies."

Afsar nodded slowly, his gaze shifting to the rows of books behind Porter, then back again. "Makes sense."

Porter picked up a small notepad from the side table, though he didn't open it yet. "Let's start at the beginning. Tell me about your childhood, Afsar. Your earliest memories. Where'd you grow up?"

"Mostly Tennessee," Afsar replied. "Water Valley. But the woods were my real home. I was out in them as often as I could be."

"And your family?"

Afsar took a breath. "Just me, my dad, and my granddad. My mom…" His voice caught slightly, but he pushed forward. "She died when I was eight."

Porter's face softened, his tone gentle. "I'm sorry. That's a tough age to lose a parent."

Afsar nodded. "It was more than tough. It wrecked me."

"What do you remember about her?"

Afsar looked down at his hands, clasped in his lap. The scent of leather and old books was grounding, comforting in a way he hadn't expected. "She was warm. Strong. Her voice was like honey—thick, soft, always wrapped in this faint accent that made every word feel like a song. She'd hum when she cooked, always something slow and sad, but she smiled a lot when she looked at me. Like I was her favorite secret."

Porter made a note, not interrupting.

"She taught me to read using old Afghan poetry books," Afsar continued. "I didn't understand half of it, but I memorized the words anyway. I wanted to make her proud. She made the world feel safe, even when it wasn't."

"And after she passed?" Porter asked, his tone even quieter now.

Afsar's throat tightened. He looked toward a bookcase rather than meet Porter's eyes.

"I didn't talk for days. Maybe weeks. I just… wandered. There was this cave in the woods behind our house. I used to go there and scream. Or cry. Or just… sit. Sometimes I imagined I was back in her arms, listening to her heartbeat. Sometimes I imagined I could still smell her perfume on the wind. Cinnamon and roses."

Porter was silent for a beat. Then he asked, "How did you come to terms with it?"

"I didn't," Afsar said. "Not really. I buried it. Told myself I had to be strong for my dad. Pretended I was fine until I almost believed it. But part of me never stopped screaming in that cave."

Porter scribbled a few words, then looked back up. "That's an incredibly honest answer, Afsar. Thank you."

Afsar shifted on the couch, not entirely comfortable with the praise. "What else do you want to know?"

Porter leaned forward, setting the notepad down. "Everything. But let's take it one layer at a time."

The next ninety minutes passed in waves—some calm, some turbulent, but all pulling from deep waters. Dr. Porter guided the conversation like a seasoned pilot steering through a storm. He circled back to memories of Afsar's mother, then forward into teenage years marked by quiet rebellion, long silences, and a simmering anger he never quite understood until recently.

They spoke of school—how Afsar aced history and literature but barely scraped through math. About his quiet leadership on the track team, his single, brief fistfight in sophomore year that got him suspended for a week. About his faith, his family's unshakable bond, and his complicated feelings about Afghanistan—his mother's homeland, and in many ways, a ghost that had always hovered nearby.

Dr. Porter probed with precision but never force. "Did you ever feel like you didn't belong?" he asked at one point.

"All the time," Afsar replied, his voice quiet. "Too brown for some crowds, too American for others. My name was always the first test."

"And how did you cope with that?"

Afsar smirked faintly. "Sarcasm. Distance. I got good at being quiet in a room without disappearing."

"Useful skill," Porter noted, scribbling. "Especially where you might be going."

As they approached the end of the session, Porter studied him with a thoughtful expression. "You've got fire, Afsar. But it's banked—controlled. Most people don't come in here knowing who they are. You do. Even if you don't always like what you find in the mirror."

Afsar tilted his head slightly, unsure whether to take that as a compliment or a warning.

Porter smiled, standing. "Let's get you out of here. You've earned a break."

He led Afsar out of the office and down the hall, the floors humming faintly underfoot with the building's central HVAC. The air had a sterile, citrusy-clean scent, sharp after the warmth of the office.

As they reached the front, the midday sun filtered through the frosted glass windows, softening the shadows in the reception area. Afsar noticed the quiet ticking of a wall clock—each second crisp, deliberate.

Porter opened the front door and gestured toward the parking lot. "You'll be hearing from someone soon. Probably not me."

Afsar extended his hand. "Thanks. For the questions. And the quiet."

Porter shook it firmly. "You're welcome. Good luck, Afsar."

With that, Afsar stepped out into the bright Nashville afternoon, the sunlight warming his face as the door closed softly behind him.

Dr. Porter had just turned back into the hallway when a side door clicked open near the rear of the corridor. Ambar stepped out first, tablet in hand, followed by Robert, his hands tucked into the pockets of a charcoal-gray blazer. The two approached Porter as he closed the door to his office with a quiet snick.

"Well?" Robert asked without preamble, his eyes sharp beneath furrowed brows. "Did he pass the sniff test?"

Porter chuckled, folding his arms. "Your instincts are still as subtle as a freight train, Robert."

Ambar gave Porter a nod of greeting, but her eyes were already searching his face for clues. "How'd he do?"

Porter leaned slightly against the wall, thoughtful. "He's... complex. Introspective. There's trauma there—deep, layered—but not the kind that shatters. The kind that forges."

Robert raised an eyebrow. "You sound like you're writing a recruitment poster."

Porter shrugged. "You wanted an evaluation. That's mine. He's emotionally intelligent, guarded but open to connection with the right prompting. Honest, sometimes painfully so. And he's carrying a history that would break most people."

"Which makes him unpredictable," Robert cut in. "And potentially unstable under pressure."

"Or incredibly resilient," Ambar countered, her voice steady. "Come on, Robert. You saw the same things I did at the interview. The way he observes, calculates. He's got a moral compass, but it doesn't get in the way of tough choices. He just needs a direction—one that matters."

Porter nodded in agreement. "He's angry. But not destructively so. In fact, it's what gives him clarity. He's not a loose cannon, Robert. He's a precision weapon—if you're careful where you point him."

Robert exhaled through his nose, jaw tight. "Still feels like a gamble."

Ambar took a step closer to him. "They all are. But this one? This one is worth it. You asked me to trust my gut. I do. And my gut says he's exactly what the Afghan Directorate needs."

There was a long pause, broken only by the distant buzz of fluorescent lights and the hum of the HVAC system. Finally, Robert gave a reluctant nod.

"Fine. Let the assessments finish. If the psych and medical clear him, he moves to training. But he's your project, Ambar. You walk him through it, and you answer for him if it goes south."

Ambar's lips lifted in a quiet, confident smile. "Gladly."

Porter pushed off the wall, adjusting the cuffs of his shirt. "You'll have my written evaluation within the hour."

As he turned to leave, Robert muttered, "God help us all if you're wrong."

Ambar watched Porter disappear down the hall, then turned toward Robert. "But what if I'm right?"

***

2015

The summer sun had just begun to set, casting warm golden light through the kitchen windows and across the worn wood of the dinner table. The comforting scent of baked chicken and garlic mashed potatoes lingered in the air, mixed with the faint aroma of fresh-cut grass drifting in from the backyard. Jack Ramos, still in his work shirt, sat at the head of the table, chewing quietly as he read over a few notes from a manila folder beside his plate.

Afsar poked at his green beans for a moment, the scrape of his fork against the plate the only sound he made. His knee bounced beneath the table, restless energy he hadn't yet figured out how to name.

Finally, he cleared his throat. "Dad?"

Jack looked up, fork paused in mid-air. "Yeah, buddy?"

Afsar sat up a little straighter. "I was thinking… I want to try out for a team at school next year. Like, maybe football or track or something."

Jack raised an eyebrow, setting his fork down. "Team sports, huh?"

Afsar nodded quickly, eyes searching his father's face for any sign of resistance. "Yeah. I've been watching them at school. Looks like something I could be good at, you know?"

Jack studied him for a long moment, then leaned back in his chair. "Well, if you're serious about it, that means you're gonna have to work for it. No showing up out of shape and expecting a spot handed to you."

"I know," Afsar said, a little too quickly. "I want to earn it."

Jack scratched his chin, the faint scrape of his nails audible in the quiet kitchen. "Alright. You want this, we start training tomorrow morning. 5:30. Rain or shine."

Afsar's eyes widened. "Wait, five-thirty in the morning?"

Jack smirked. "That's when the work gets done. You want to play like a man? You train like one."

There was a pause, the kind where the air feels like it's holding its breath. Afsar glanced at his plate, then back at his father, a grin slowly forming.

"Okay," he said with a nod. "I'm in."

Jack picked up his fork again, his expression softening with pride. "Good. Let's see what you're made of, son."

The cicadas started up outside the window, a steady hum beneath the stillness of the evening. Afsar reached for a second helping, already feeling a spark inside him—like something had just shifted into place.

The next morning broke early, the horizon still painted in hues of purple and deep blue when Afsar's alarm buzzed on his nightstand. He groaned, slapped at the button, and sat up slowly, eyes gritty with sleep. The house was quiet except for the soft creak of the wooden floors under his feet. As he stepped outside, a damp wave of cool morning air wrapped around him, the scent of dew-drenched grass thick and earthy.

Jack was already waiting in the driveway, dressed in a faded Army T-shirt, stopwatch around his neck, and coffee mug in hand. His breath puffed in small clouds against the early chill.

"Morning, sunshine," Jack called. "You stretch already or do we gotta waste time on that?"

Afsar blinked, still waking up. "I just got out here…"

"Wrong answer," Jack barked with a grin that didn't quite reach his eyes. "When I say five-thirty, I mean *ready* at five-thirty. Let's go—high knees to the stop sign. Move it!"

Afsar startled into motion, stumbling into the run down the gravel road, the small stones biting at his sneakers. His breath puffed with each stride, lungs protesting, legs awkward and heavy.

"Pump your arms! Knees up! This ain't a funeral march!" Jack shouted, jogging behind him.

By the time they returned, Afsar was panting hard, sweat starting to bead along his hairline as the sun crested over the trees. Jack handed him a water bottle.

"Good," he said. "Now we do ladder drills. Don't trip or I'll make you start over."

And so it went. Every morning like clockwork, Jack dragged him through the paces with the stern patience of a drill instructor: pushups until his arms burned, footwork patterns drawn in chalk on the driveway, cone drills set up in the backyard, and long runs through the wooded trail behind the house.

The smell of pine and sweat became familiar to Afsar, as did the taste of salt on his lips and the ache in his legs that never fully went away. The slap of sneakers against pavement, the clink of Jack's stopwatch, and the bark of his voice became part of the soundtrack of that summer.

One morning, about three weeks in, Afsar collapsed on the lawn after a set of uphill sprints. He lay on the damp grass, chest heaving, arms flung wide.

"I can't feel my legs," he groaned.

"You'll thank me when you're outrunning linebackers next year," Jack said, tossing him a towel. "Now get up. You've got two more rounds."

Afsar groaned louder, but he rolled over, grinning despite the exhaustion.

He was starting to get faster. Stronger. And even Jack—though he wouldn't say it—was starting to notice.

The sun hung low in the sky, casting long golden rays through the thinning summer trees. The morning air was thick with humidity, wrapping around them like a damp towel. Jack stood at the edge of the field, stopwatch in hand, watching as Afsar powered through another set of wind sprints, his shirt soaked through with sweat, his breath ragged but determined.

Jack nodded to himself, impressed. "That's it. Drive those knees, finish strong!"

Afsar crossed the line marked in the grass and bent over, hands on his knees, gulping air. His face was flushed, shirt clinging to his back, sneakers coated in dust.

Jack walked over, handed him a bottle of water, and said in a quiet voice, "Your mother would've been proud of this."

The words hit harder than a punch.

Afsar froze, the bottle hovering just below his lips. His breath slowed, shoulders rising and falling as he stared somewhere past Jack, past the field, past the moment. A shadow passed behind his eyes. The letter—crisp but yellowing, folded neatly—flashed across his mind again like a wound reopened:

He didn't say anything. Just nodded once, jaw tightening.

Jack saw it—the way his son's jaw set like stone, how his eyes hardened just a little more—but didn't press.

Afsar took a long drink, wiped his mouth with the back of his arm, and without another word, turned and jogged back to the starting line. Another round. More wind sprints. More silence. More pain to burn.

He wasn't running for the team anymore. He was running from ghosts.

Chapter 7

The late summer sun filtered through the blinds in Afsar's room, casting slatted shadows across the floor. He sat on the edge of his bed, scrolling aimlessly through his phone, the silence of the afternoon interrupted only by the quiet hum of cicadas outside. His duffel bag, half-packed with gym clothes and notebooks, lay open on the floor. He had started preparing himself for a future with or without a call.

Then, the phone rang.

He glanced at the screen. *Ambar.*

His stomach tightened. He answered quickly, trying to keep his tone neutral. "Hello?"

"Hey, Afsar," Ambar's voice came through bright, even, and calm. "You busy?"

"No, just, uh… hanging out. Thinking." He stood up and began pacing slowly, his fingers fidgeting with the hem of his t-shirt. "What's up?"

"Well," she said, drawing it out just enough to make him stop walking. "I wanted to be the first to tell you—officially—you're in."

Afsar blinked. "I'm what?"

"You're in, Afsar," she repeated, a smile in her voice. "You passed everything. Robert signed off yesterday, and the greenlight came through this morning."

He sat back down, hard. The room suddenly felt smaller. His breath caught for just a second before he could speak. "So… this is really happening?"

"It is. You're going to be part of the Agency's Afghan Directorate Initiative," she said, tone softening. "I knew from the beginning, but it's good to see everyone else catch up."

He let out a quiet breath, part disbelief, part relief. Outside, a breeze stirred the trees, and the faint scent of cut grass drifted through the open window. "What happens next?"

"I'll send you a packet with the official documents. Training starts in six weeks," she replied. "Between now and then, there's a lot of prep. We'll help you with everything. But today—today, just enjoy this moment."

He leaned back, staring up at the ceiling. The ceiling fan spun lazily above him. He could still hear the faint echo of his dad's voice from their morning workouts, still feel the heat of that hunt years ago, still taste the salt of sweat and resolve.

"I'm in," he repeated, quieter this time, like he still didn't fully believe it. "Thank you, Ambar."

"You earned it," she said, then added with a teasing lilt, "But don't go soft on me now. This is just the beginning."

Afsar cracked a smile. "I wouldn't dream of it."

From the other end, she laughed gently, the kind of laugh that said she knew exactly what this meant to him.

Afsar pulled into the driveway just after four, the Mustang's exhaust still hanging in the humid afternoon air. His backpack slung lazily over one shoulder, he spotted the telltale white FedEx box propped against the front door.

His pulse quickened.

He picked it up—light but packed tightly, his name and address printed cleanly across the top. *Langley return address*, no overt branding. Just like she said it would be.

The front door creaked open. Inside, the house smelled faintly of old wood, detergent, and the lingering scent of his dad's morning coffee. He tossed his backpack near the couch, set the box on the dining table, then ducked into the kitchen.

He popped two slices of bread into the toaster and grabbed the peanut butter. While spreading it, he kept glancing back toward the table like it might vanish if left unattended. As the toaster clicked off, he slapped the sandwich together and carried it, along with a glass of milk, to the dining table.

With his foot, he nudged a chair out and sat down. He peeled back the packing tape carefully, like unwrapping something sacred.

Inside: a padded folder marked *For Recipient Only*. A letter on thick paper with government headers. A sleek, thin booklet titled *Introduction to Field Operations – Directorate Program, Afghanistan*. A checklist. A plain black lanyard with a plastic badge holder—empty. And a thumb drive, unmarked.

He took a bite of his sandwich, chewing slowly as his eyes scanned the introductory letter. Words like *confidential*, *non-transferable*, and *background verification* leapt off the page.

Then the front door opened.

Heavy boots on the wooden floor. A tired sigh.

Jack Ramos walked in, his work shirt smudged with the day's labor, a thermos dangling from one calloused hand.

"Hey, bud," he called, setting his keys in the bowl by the door. "You beat me home."

Afsar straightened up instinctively. "Yeah. School let out early."

Jack walked toward the dining room, loosening his belt slightly, pausing when he saw the open package on the table.

He nodded toward it. "That what I think it is?"

Afsar swallowed the last bit of sandwich and nodded. "Came today. Three days after the call."

Jack walked closer, picking up the *Introduction to Field Operations* booklet. He flipped it open, scanning the inside cover, then looked up. "They don't waste time."

"Nope." Afsar's voice held a quiet mix of nerves and pride.

Jack pulled out a chair across from his son and eased into it, still holding the booklet. "You read it yet?"

"Just started. There's a lot." Afsar tapped the thumb drive. "She said there'd be videos and some training modules."

Jack raised an eyebrow. "You know what this means, right?"

Afsar met his father's gaze. "Yeah. I think I do." His voice was even. "It's real now."

Jack leaned back, exhaling through his nose. He set the booklet down gently, fingers drumming on the table once before he spoke again.

"I figured when that call came, this house was gonna feel different."

Afsar looked around. It did. The silence was heavier, denser. Charged with something unsaid.

But before either could speak again, the sound of a notification dinged from the laptop inside the box, drawing both of their attention.

Jack gave a half-smile. "Well… better see what your new boss has to say."

Dinner was simple—leftover pot roast, mashed potatoes, and green beans from the night before. Jack loaded their plates while Afsar cleared the documents off the dining table and set them on the nearby sideboard. The FedEx box now sat closed, tucked beside the unused laptop.

They ate mostly in silence at first, the clink of forks against ceramic the only sound in the room. Afsar shoveled in a bite of green beans, still distracted by the unopened laptop and the thought of what might be waiting on the drive.

Jack took a long sip from his glass of sweet tea, then set it down with a soft clunk. "You ever hear much about what it was like over there?" he asked, not looking directly at Afsar.

Afsar paused, his fork halfway to his mouth. "You mean Afghanistan?"

Jack nodded.

"Just bits and pieces," Afsar said carefully. "You didn't talk about it much."

Jack wiped his mouth with a napkin and leaned back in his chair, looking out the kitchen window into the dusky backyard. "It was beautiful," he said after a moment. "Which sounds strange, I know. But parts of it were… raw. Mountains that looked like the bones of the earth, valleys so quiet you'd swear God was still whispering in them."

Afsar's eyes lingered on his father's face.

"But it was hard," Jack continued, his voice low. "Dust so fine it got into your teeth. Days so hot the soles of your boots felt like they'd melt. And the people? Complicated. Proud. Cautious. A lot like here in some ways, just different rules." He glanced at Afsar then. "You learn fast who's your friend and who'll sell you for a goat."

Afsar didn't say anything. He just nodded and returned to pushing the last of the potatoes around his plate.

"Had a few close calls," Jack added. "IEDs. Snipers. But most of the time… it was waiting. Wondering. Trying not to do something stupid." He gave a quiet chuckle. "I was young. Dumb. Thought I knew everything."

Afsar gave a small grin. "Guess that runs in the family."

Jack smirked. "Guess so."

They finished the rest of the meal in more comfortable silence. After clearing the plates, Afsar finally walked back over to the table and opened the laptop. As it booted, a soft chime rang out—a notification flashing in the corner.

Secure Email: ACCESS AUTH GRANTED — Time-sensitive Briefing Materials Ready.

Afsar clicked it open, scanning the header quickly. Below it, a short line from Ashlynn:

Glad you got the package :) Let me know if you need help setting anything up. — Ash

Afsar smiled faintly and pulled out his phone, tapping a reply.

Got the package. Booting up now. Appreciate you. — A

Jack stood behind him, arms crossed, watching the screen. "So. This is it."

Afsar nodded. "Yeah."

Jack rested a hand briefly on his son's shoulder. "Then we better make sure you're ready."

The house buzzed with quiet excitement and the faint smell of starch and fresh cologne. In the back bedroom, Afsar adjusted the stiff collar of his dress shirt in the mirror, running a hand over his neatly parted hair. His graduation gown hung on the back of the door, already pressed and ready. A blue honor cord draped across the foot of the bed. The last three weeks had passed in a blur—final exams, government paperwork that felt more endless than the tests, and long late-night texts that had turned into phone calls, then into something… warmer. Ashlynn had become more than a voice on the other end of a message. She was part of his day now. A constant, confident energy that kept him sharp and made him laugh when the weight of everything got too heavy.

A knock echoed through the house.

Jack's voice called out from the hallway. "I got it!"

Afsar listened as his father opened the front door, the hinges creaking slightly. Then came Jack's voice again, this time with that familiar twang of amused approval.

"Well now, look who we have here. You must be Ashlynn."

Her bright voice carried through. "Hi, Mr. Ramos. Sorry if I'm early. I just wanted to beat traffic and make sure Afsar had someone there to cheer obnoxiously from the crowd."

Jack chuckled. "He'll appreciate that. Come on in."

Footsteps moved through the house as Jack led her in. Afsar stepped out into the hallway just as they rounded the corner. Ashlynn looked radiant— summer dress in a pale shade of coral, hair tucked behind one ear, eyes lighting up the moment she saw him.

"Well, look at you," she said with a smile. "Mr. Graduate."

He smirked. "Give me a couple hours. I've got to walk the stage first."

Ashlynn took a step closer, brushing some lint from his shoulder. "You clean up nice. Didn't think you'd have it in you."

"Please," Afsar shot back. "You saw my eighth-grade church banquet photo."

"Exactly."

Jack grinned at the banter, then nodded toward the kitchen. "I've got some coffee brewing if either of you want some before we head out."

"Love some," Ashlynn said, already stepping that way. "Black. Like my sense of humor."

Afsar followed her with a half-smile, still adjusting the fit of his shirt, and feeling, for the first time in a long time, like the next chapter might be worth turning the page for.

The sun was out in full force by the time they reached the campus parking lot, the asphalt radiating heat even in the early afternoon. Students in blue gowns and flat mortarboards hustled across the quad, families trailing behind with bouquets and beaming pride.

In Jack's old Silverado, the mood was light. Ashlynn rode shotgun, her legs tucked beneath her as she scrolled through her phone for the schedule of events.

"You nervous?" she asked, glancing back at Afsar in the rear seat.

Afsar shrugged, tugging at his collar. "Not about walking across the stage. I'm more worried about tripping in front of a thousand people and living in infamy on TikTok."

Jack laughed as he turned onto the main road. "If you fall, son, just pop up like you meant to do it. Confidence is half the game."

Ashlynn turned, grinning. "Or just moonwalk the rest of the way. Own it."

"Yeah, sure," Afsar replied dryly. "Because what screams government recruit like Michael Jackson moves at graduation."

They pulled into the university lot and navigated the chaos of proud parents and wandering students. After checking in and being corralled by staff toward the staging area, Afsar broke off, exchanging a quick look with Jack and Ashlynn.

"You two know where to sit?"

Jack nodded. "We'll find you. I'm loud. And she's louder."

Ashlynn winked. "You'll hear us."

Inside the fieldhouse, the air buzzed with excitement and the murmuring of hundreds of attendees packed into bleachers. Folding chairs lined the floor, a sea of navy gowns shimmering under fluorescent lights.

Banners hung from the rafters: *Middle Tennessee State University — Class of 2024*

The commencement ceremony opened with an a cappella version of the national anthem, followed by greetings from the dean and the reading of academic honors. Then, a renowned heart surgeon—Dr. Kavita Raman—stepped to the podium. She was small in stature but carried herself with gravitas, her voice calm and precise.

"I've held the human heart in my hands more times than I can count," she began, "and each time, I'm reminded of how fragile and miraculous life is. Your education, your achievements—those are the bones of your success. But your heart, your courage, your resilience… that's what will determine your legacy."

The speech was inspiring, but Afsar barely heard it. His thoughts kept drifting—toward what lay ahead, toward the next phase of the journey Ambar and Robert had set into motion, and toward the pair of hazel eyes now scanning the program in the crowd.

Then came the roll call.

"Afsar Ramos!"

His name rang through the PA system like a bell. He stood, spine straight, and walked across the stage under the lights. The applause was polite, restrained—until, from the far right side of the audience:

"YEAH, AFSAR!"

"WOOOOO! THAT'S MY BOY!"

Ashlynn's high-pitched cheer followed Jack's booming shout. A few rows in front turned to look, smiling in amusement.

Afsar didn't blush, didn't flinch. He just smiled and tipped his head slightly in their direction as he took his diploma and shook hands with the dean.

Unseen to all but the most observant, a solitary woman stood in the back near the exit doors—Ambar Shoeston. Dressed in muted tones, she blended into the scenery like a shadow. But her sharp eyes never left Afsar. Her lips curved into the faintest smile—not just of pride, but of certainty.

This was the right one.

The summer sun was just starting to rise, casting a warm amber glow over the tarmac at Nashville International Airport. The terminal was already alive with the usual buzz of rolling suitcases, echoing announcements, and sleepy-eyed travelers clutching coffee cups like lifelines.

Jack pulled the truck into the departures lane, easing into a spot near the curb. Afsar sat in the back seat, duffel bag across his lap, while Ashlynn looked over at him from the front, trying to hide the emotion brewing in her chest.

Jack killed the engine and turned to look back at his son. "Well," he said gruffly, "this is it."

Afsar took a breath and opened the door. The cool, conditioned air of the terminal spilled out as he stepped onto the curb. Jack and Ashlynn joined him, each grabbing a piece of his luggage.

Ashlynn was the first to speak. "You sure you packed everything?" she asked, trying to keep her voice light. "Socks, charger, toothpaste, dangerously charming smile?"

Afsar gave her a crooked grin. "I'm traveling light. Just bringing what matters."

She nodded, then reached in to hug him tightly, her cheek pressed against his chest. "Be careful, okay? I mean it."

"I will," he said softly, his arms firm around her.

Jack stood a few steps back, arms crossed, eyes a little red though he didn't say anything at first. When Afsar finally turned to him, the two just stared at each other for a moment.

"Come here," Jack muttered, his voice catching.

They embraced, hard and silent at first. Jack's hand came up and gripped the back of his son's head like he had when Afsar was small.

"I don't know where exactly you're goin'," Jack said, voice low near Afsar's ear, "but I know why. And I'm proud of you. Just… keep your head on straight. You hear me?"

Afsar nodded against his shoulder. "I will, Dad."

They stood like that a beat longer, clinging to a moment that neither wanted to end.

When they finally stepped apart, Jack sniffed and nodded. "Alright then."

Afsar slung his duffel over his shoulder, gave Ashlynn one last look—a soft smile that said everything without words and a kiss—then turned toward the terminal.

He didn't look back.

He moved through the automatic doors, merged with the line at TSA, and slowly disappeared into the crowd. Ashlynn watched him go until he was swallowed by the checkpoint. Jack stood beside her, silent and unmoving.

The sun climbed higher behind them, casting long shadows behind their still forms.

***

2002

The old fan spun lazily above them, its rhythmic creaking barely covering the quiet murmur of their voices. The room smelled faintly of dust and cedar, the scent of summer clinging to the walls. A single candle flickered next to the bed, casting a warm glow over the worn cloth hanging from the walls.

Afsoon sat cross-legged on the edge of the bed, her scarf loosely draped over her shoulders, her eyes fixed on the boy she had come to love more than anything in the world. Jamal leaned against the headboard, a hint of stubble on his chin, his hand brushing hers as if afraid she'd vanish if he let go.

"I hate sneaking around like this," she whispered. "I hate hiding every piece of my life from them."

"I know," Jamal said, his voice low. "But we're not going to hide much longer."

Her eyes widened. "You really mean it?"

He nodded. "I've got everything planned. One bus ticket from Khost to Kabul, then we stay with my cousin near Wazir Akbar Khan until we find our own place. I've already spoken to him. He'll help."

Afsoon exhaled, trying to imagine the city lights, the noise, the freedom. It seemed unreal, like a dream she hadn't dared to speak aloud.

"What if they come after me?" she asked. "You know what my father's like. What my uncles are like."

"I won't let them take you back," Jamal said fiercely. "I'll protect you. We'll be gone before they even know you left."

A silence fell between them. Not empty—heavy, meaningful. Afsoon leaned her head on his shoulder.

"I love you," she said softly.

Jamal turned to kiss her forehead. "And I love you. Enough to risk everything."

She smiled, but it trembled at the corners. "We'll need to leave soon. Before Eid. They're already watching me too closely."

Jamal reached under the bed and pulled out a small cloth bag. Inside was some cash, a forged ID, and a phone with a Kabul SIM card. He placed it in her lap gently.

"Our life starts soon."

Afsoon stared at it, then back at him, her heart pounding.

"Promise me this isn't just a dream."

He reached out, took her hands, and kissed her knuckles.

"I promise. Kabul's waiting for us."

The wind rustled the curtains as the moon climbed higher over the rooftops of Spera. Jamal lit the small gas lamp beside the bed, dimming the bulb so the light wouldn't seep through the cracks in the shutters. They sat cross-legged on the mattress, a map of the region unfolded between them, dog-eared and marked with circles and arrows.

Afsoon traced the route with her finger. "So we meet here, by the orchard fence behind the mosque. After the evening prayers?"

Jamal nodded. "Exactly. I'll already have the motorbike waiting. It's less suspicious than the bus at first. We'll ride to Khost, then catch the late-night bus to Kabul from there."

"And your cousin… he won't tell anyone?"

"He's like a brother. He owes me from when his father passed. He knows what's at stake."

Afsoon looked down at her hands. "I haven't packed much. Just a few clothes, some books, and the necklace my mother gave me before she got sick."

Jamal reached over and gently turned her chin toward him. "Take what matters. Everything else, we'll build together."

She swallowed, her eyes stinging. "I'm scared, Jamal."

"I know." He reached for her hand. "I am too. But what scares me more is staying here, watching them cage you like your dreams don't matter. Like your voice doesn't matter."

Afsoon gave a sad smile, eyes full of love. "You always know exactly what to say."

He smirked. "Only with you."

She lay back on the mattress, hands folded behind her head, staring at the cracked ceiling. "It's late. If I go now, someone might see me…"

Jamal sat up straighter, suddenly alert. "Do you want to go? I'll walk you back if you feel safer at home."

"No," she said quickly, turning to him. "No. I want to stay. Just for tonight."

Jamal hesitated for a moment, then nodded. "Alright. You can have the bed. I'll take the floor."

Afsoon reached out and caught his wrist. "We've been planning our whole future together. I think I can handle sharing a pillow."

His cheeks flushed slightly, but he smiled and nodded. "Okay."

They slid under the thin blanket together, their backs to the wall, facing one another in the pale glow of the lamp. He tucked a stray strand of hair behind her ear, and she rested her forehead against his.

"Promise me, Jamal," she whispered. "No matter what happens, we don't turn back."

"I promise," he said. "Not even death will stop me from getting you to Kabul."

Their hands remained entwined between them as the room fell quiet—two hearts beating against a world that didn't want them together.

Afsoon lay at the edge of the small bed, her arms wrapped around him. Jamal pulled back the thin blanket and gave her a reassuring smile.

"You can take the side by the wall," he said gently. "It's warmer there."

She nodded, brushing her hair back and slipping under the covers beside him. The dim glow of the lamp on his nightstand cast soft shadows across the room.

For a moment, they lay still, facing each other in the quiet.

"I still can't believe we're really doing this," Afsoon whispered, her voice barely audible. "Leaving everything behind."

Jamal reached out and gently tucked a strand of hair behind her ear. "It's not everything. It's just… the part that's kept you from being free. The rest—your dreams, your heart—you're bringing all that with you. And I'll protect it."

Her eyes shimmered as they searched his face. "What if we get caught?"

"Then we run faster," he said with a playful smile, then added more seriously, "We'll be smart. Careful. And no matter what happens, I'll never leave your side."

She reached out and took his hand under the blanket, threading her fingers through his. "I love you, Jamal."

He leaned in, his forehead resting against hers. "I love you too, Afsoon. More than this town. More than anything."

They lay there, cocooned in each other's presence, hearts pounding not from fear—but from the hope of something better, something new. As the night deepened, Afsoon rested her head on Jamal's chest, and the two started to embrace and move with the passion of two starry-eyed lovers facing an uncertain future together, holding tightly to the promise of freedom just beyond the horizon.

Chapter 8

The wheels of the plane screeched against the tarmac as Afsar's flight touched down in Las Vegas, a sudden jolt shaking him from his nap. The familiar *ding* of the seatbelt sign echoed through the cabin, and soon the aircraft was taxiing toward the gate under the blazing Nevada sun. The desert heat shimmered off the runways in hazy waves.

As Afsar stepped off the plane and into Harry Ried International Airport, he took a deep breath, feeling the buzz of the city even inside the terminal. Slot machines chimed in greeting. The air smelled like recycled air and perfume, tinged with the distant scent of fried food.

He moved toward baggage claim with purpose, scanning the crowd. Then he saw her—Ambar, standing near the carousel, dark sunglasses over her eyes, a slim black leather jacket over a sand-colored blouse and jeans. She offered him a subtle smile and a nod.

"Welcome to Vegas," she said as he approached.

Afsar grinned. "Thanks. Never thought I'd be meeting a federal handler next to a luggage belt."

"Well, the Agency spares no expense," she deadpanned, glancing toward the carousel. "Just wait until you see the buffet."

Afsar chuckled as his duffel bag slid into view. He reached out, grabbed it in one motion, and slung it over his shoulder.

"Come on," Ambar said. "Car's this way."

They walked through the terminal, weaving past flocks of tourists in matching T-shirts and over-eager gamblers clutching plastic yard drinks. Outside, the heat hit like a furnace, dry and relentless. The scent of hot asphalt and engine exhaust clung to the air.

Ambar led him into the parking structure and to a silver Nissan Altima parked near the stairwell.

"Not exactly a blacked-out SUV," Afsar noted, tossing his bag in the backseat.

"Discretion is part of the job," Ambar replied, slipping behind the wheel. "Besides, you blend in a lot easier when you don't look like you're heading to a government sting."

The drive off the Strip was quiet, the neon chaos of Las Vegas Boulevard giving way to industrial blocks and low-slung shopping centers. Finally, they pulled into the parking garage of the Silverton Station Casino, tucked away off Blue Diamond Road—a small, unassuming place frequented by locals and those who didn't want to be noticed.

Ambar shifted the car into park, then reached into the center console and pulled out a plastic card key.

"You're in Room 917. I'm in 919," she said, handing him the key. "Keep it close. Don't lose it. Don't draw attention. We keep it low profile, okay?"

Afsar took the card and studied it for a second before tucking it into his pocket. "Got it."

She looked at him for a moment longer, as if weighing something, then added, "Grab some rest. We'll debrief in an hour. And Afsar?"

"Yeah?"

"Whatever this place looks like on the outside, this is your first step into something very real. Don't let the casino lights fool you."

Afsar nodded, his expression turning serious. "Understood."

And with that, he opened the door, stepped out into the stale heat of the parking garage, and walked toward the elevator, key card in hand.

The Silverton buffet glowed under soft amber lighting, filled with the hum of quiet conversation, clinking silverware, and the muted whirl of dessert machines. Afsar followed Ambar down the line, tray in hand, surveying the spread—carved prime rib, crab legs stacked like firewood, an unnecessarily large taco station, and a modest international section that looked like it hadn't been updated since the mid-2000s.

He scooped a portion of garlic mashed potatoes onto his plate, then glanced at Ambar. "You sure this place isn't a front for a government ops center?"

She smirked, tonging some roasted vegetables onto her own tray. "You'd be surprised how much good intel gets picked up in places like this. Boozy businessmen love to brag at buffets."

They found a quiet corner booth near a fake waterfall and sat opposite each other. Afsar dug into his food, clearly famished after the flight.

"So," Ambar said, stabbing a green bean with surgical precision, "you and Ashlynn. That seems to be heating up."

Afsar looked up, half a bite into his chicken. "You've got spies watching me already?"

She shrugged. "Not officially. But a good handler knows how to read between the lines."

He smirked. "Yeah, it's… something. Unexpected, I guess. She gets me in a way that's rare. Like I don't have to explain everything twice."

Ambar's eyes softened. "That's not nothing."

"It's more than I expected, honestly. Especially with everything going on." He leaned back a little, wiping his mouth. "I think she knows there's something about this I can't tell her. And she's not pushing. That scares me a little."

"Good people usually do," Ambar said. "They give space, not because they don't care—but because they do."

He nodded thoughtfully.

They ate in silence for a few moments, the sounds of slot machines faint through the walls. Afsar spoke again, quieter this time.

"You keeping up with what's happening in Iran?" he asked.

Ambar looked up from her plate. "Of course. Proxy militias tightening their grip, currency tanking, old guard getting desperate. That what's on your mind?"

"That and Russia throwing their weight around in Central Asia again. Lotta people pretending the Cold War ended."

"It didn't," she said simply. "It just changed names."

Afsar let out a dry laugh. "Guess I'll be learning all about that soon."

Ambar's eyes held his for a beat. "You already are."

A beat passed between them, quiet but charged.

Then she lifted her glass of iced tea. "To new chapters."

Afsar raised his own. "And whatever the hell this chapter's called."

They clinked glasses with a soft *tap*, two people on the edge of something much larger than either could name just yet.

The next morning, Vegas shimmered beneath a gauzy desert sun. By the time Afsar and Ambar stepped out of the casino, the heat was already clinging to their skin like a second shirt. Afsar wore sunglasses and a ballcap low over his brow, backpack slung casually over one shoulder. Ambar, in fitted jeans and a light blouse, walked with purpose.

"First stop," she said, unlocking the car with a chirp, "is for my sanity. You can't come to Vegas without seeing the damn Hoover Dam."

Afsar grinned as he slid into the passenger seat. "Let me guess, next you'll tell me we're hitting up Area 51."

"One conspiracy at a time, rookie," she quipped.

They reached the dam just after mid-morning, the Colorado River a deep, glassy ribbon far below. The air smelled faintly of hot rock and dry concrete. Afsar stood near the edge, peering over the side.

"Jesus," he murmured. "This is… massive."

"It's supposed to make you feel small," Ambar said from behind him. "That's the point. Big engineering, big ambition. Depression-era flex."

He turned to her. "Kinda like Vegas itself."

She gave him a crooked smile. "Exactly. This whole state is built on illusion and grit."

Over the next couple of days, they hit the Strip for just long enough to gawk at the spectacle—the Bellagio fountains erupting in sync with Sinatra, the replica Eiffel Tower, the endless buzz of slot machines and overpriced cocktails. Ambar never let them linger too long. She steered them clear of the tourist traps, taking back roads and weird little side stops.

They watched the sunset from Red Rock Canyon, the orange cliffs glowing like coals as the sky melted into purple and gold.

"Never thought I'd say this," Afsar said, hands in his pockets, "but this doesn't feel like training."

Ambar leaned against a rock beside him. "It's not. This is the last time your life will be yours. This…

stretch of freedom. Sightseeing. Breathing. No handlers, no protocols. Just air and space. Enjoy it."

He glanced at her. "That's… a little ominous."

"It's the truth."

They ate street tacos from a truck parked behind a biker bar on Fremont Street, watched a light show on the canopy overhead, and made quiet jokes about tourists losing it at craps tables. Afsar soaked in every moment like he knew it was about to end.

On the second night, they stood at the edge of the strip, looking out across the city from a high rooftop lounge. The wind tousled Afsar's hair, carrying with it a faint scent of smoke, liquor, and heat.

Ambar leaned over the railing beside him. "Tomorrow, it changes. You ready?"

Afsar stared out at the glittering sprawl. "No."

She looked at him sidelong.

"But I will be," he added. "You'll see."

Ambar nodded once, satisfied.

"Good," she said. "Because ready or not, here it comes."

The sun hadn't yet crested the desert horizon when Ambar pulled into the private terminal at the airport. The lot was quiet, the kind of quiet that felt out of place in a city like Vegas. No flashing lights. No noise. Just the low hum of the engine and the occasional creak of the car settling.

Afsar sat in the passenger seat, duffel bag on his lap, eyes fixed ahead.

"You sleep at all?" Ambar asked, throwing the car into park.

"Couple hours." He looked over. "Didn't really need more."

She studied him for a second. "Nerves?"

He smirked faintly. "No. I'm ready."

Ambar gave him a short nod. "Good. You'll need that."

They got out in silence, the desert chill still lingering in the air. She walked him to the terminal door, where a man in a dark suit with mirrored sunglasses waited, clipboard in hand. With a brief exchange of names and a signature, Afsar was waved through the small security checkpoint and toward the tarmac.

"Remember," Ambar said, pulling him aside before he reached the plane, "everything you've done so far was the audition. What's ahead? That's the job. No more handholding."

Afsar squared his shoulders. "I'm not expecting any."

She looked him up and down one last time, a flicker of pride—or maybe concern—crossing her features. Then she reached out and gave his shoulder a firm squeeze.

"You're going to do just fine, Afsar."

He gave her a nod and turned toward the small, unmarked jet.

The flight was quick. No stewardess. No announcements. Just the quiet thrum of engines and the view of endless desert crawling beneath him.

When the wheels touched down, the plane taxied to a barren stretch of tarmac surrounded by scrub brush and distant mountains. A single black SUV waited near a hangar, parked at an angle like it owned the place.

As Afsar stepped off the stairs and onto the concrete, the door to the SUV opened.

Out stepped a man.

He was tall—easily over six feet—with arms like steel beams crossed over his chest. His fitted muscle tee strained slightly across his broad shoulders, and his cargo pants looked tactical rather than casual. A long scar traced the left side of his jawline, and his close-cropped hair bristled in the desert wind.

The man looked Afsar over like he was sizing up a new recruit—because he was.

Then, a crooked grin spread across his face.

"Welcome to your new home," the man said, voice gravelly but amused. "Welcome to Area 51."

***

2017

The desert sun beat down on the rows of teenagers filing off the tour bus, their chatter buzzing like cicadas as they hit the parking lot of the Mob Museum in downtown Las Vegas. Afsar, now fifteen, stepped off last, slinging his small backpack over one shoulder. He wore a faded MTSU ball cap low over his brow and sunglasses that did little to mask the curiosity dancing behind his eyes.

"Alright, y'all, stick together!" Mr. Garner, their history teacher, called out as he adjusted his straw hat and clipboard. "We're starting here and working our way through the city—Mob Museum, then Fremont

Street, then back to the Strip for the fountains. Eyes open, ears open."

"Bet the mob had more fun here than we're about to," Afsar muttered under his breath.

His best friend, Brian, nudged him with an elbow. "C'mon, man. You don't think it's wild that some guys ran this whole town like their own video game?"

Afsar gave a half-smile. "It is wild. Just doesn't seem so long ago. That's what gets me."

Inside the museum, Afsar stuck close to the front of the group, listening intently to the exhibit guide explain how organized crime shaped Las Vegas. He lingered at the artifacts—Tommy guns, black-and-white mugshots, even the replica electric chair. He read every placard twice.

"I swear," Brian whispered, leaning over to him as they stood in front of Bugsy Siegel's timeline, "you act like you're trying to write a book about this stuff."

Afsar shrugged. "I just like knowing how people think. What makes 'em dangerous. What makes 'em predictable."

Brian gave him a sideways glance. "That's kinda dark, bro."

"Maybe," Afsar said, "but it's useful."

Later, the class roamed Fremont Street, the lights buzzing to life under the setting sun. Afsar didn't gamble—none of them could—but he watched the street performers, the drunk tourists, the dealers in pressed uniforms. He noticed how everyone moved with a rhythm, like there were rules, even in the chaos.

The next day, the bus rumbled along the edge of Route 66, kicking up desert dust behind them as they stopped at a kitschy diner outside Kingman, Arizona. Chrome signs, vintage booths, and old Route 66 postcards lined the walls.

"This is like something outta Fallout," Brian said, flipping through a menu.

"Yeah," Afsar said, staring out the window. "Except the apocalypse already happened here—it just kept going."

After milkshakes and burgers, the group hit the road again, snaking their way toward the Grand Canyon. A hush fell over the bus as they approached the rim, every kid pressing their face to the windows. Afsar didn't say a word. When they finally stepped off and stood at the edge, he walked a few paces away from the others.

The canyon stretched endlessly before him—raw, ancient, untouchable. He stared into it for a long time, silent.

Mrs. Haskins, the assistant chaperone, walked up beside him. "Beautiful, isn't it?"

Afsar nodded slowly. "Yeah. Makes you feel like… everything else is kinda small, doesn't it?"

She smiled at him. "You're more thoughtful than most kids your age."

He didn't answer right away. "I just think some things are worth feeling quiet about."

Back on the bus, as the sun dipped below the horizon and cast shadows over the canyon walls, Afsar leaned back in his seat, arms crossed behind his head. The laughter and chatter of his classmates buzzed around him like static.

But his mind was elsewhere—still staring into the vastness, still calculating something bigger than he could explain.

The last day of the trip brought them to the Hoover Dam, a concrete colossus carved into the canyon, humming with history and power. The students filed out of the bus, necks craned and jaws slack as they took in the sheer magnitude of it.

"Whoa," Brian muttered, stepping beside Afsar at the railing. "This thing's huge."

Afsar tilted his head, eyes narrowing as he studied the dam's immense curvature and the water it held back. "It's like they built a wall against nature itself," he said. "And they're just daring it to push back."

Mr. Garner strolled over, adjusting his lanyard. "Now this is an engineering marvel, folks. Holds back the Colorado River. Provides power to three states. Took thousands of men and five years to build. They don't make 'em like this anymore."

"Wonder what's down at the bottom," a kid behind them said.

"Pressure," Afsar replied without turning. "A lot of it."

They laughed, took pictures, and filed through the dam's interior on a guided tour, gawking at the massive turbines and cool underground tunnels. Afsar trailed near the back of the group, hands in his pockets, soaking in every detail with quiet intensity.

On the way back to Vegas, the bus hummed with sleepy teenagers, worn out from the whirlwind week. The driver, a wiry older man with sunglasses and a ball cap pulled low, picked up the microphone as they rolled past McCarran International Airport.

"Alright, kids," he said, voice crackling through the speakers, "pay attention. See that plain beige building on the edge of the tarmac? Right there, with no signs?"

A few kids glanced up lazily, some still half-dozing.

"That," the driver continued, "is a J.A.N.E.T. terminal. Stands for 'Just Another Non-Existent Terminal.' It's where government contractors board unmarked planes and fly out to a little place you might've heard of—Area 51."

A murmur of interest spread across the bus. A few kids sat up straighter.

"No way," Brian said, elbowing Afsar. "That for real?"

Afsar stared out the window, watching the nondescript structure pass by. It looked like nothing. That was the point. "Yeah," he said quietly. "It's real."

"Think aliens are out there?" a girl called from a few seats back.

The bus erupted into laughter, the moment turning into a joke, a ghost story for teenagers on a long drive home.

But Afsar kept looking out the window, eyes fixed on the terminal long after it disappeared from view, his mind already peeling back layers.

Some places didn't need a name to carry weight.

Some doors only opened for the right kind of silence.

Chapter 9

The knock wasn't gentle.

BAM BAM BAM.

Afsar jerked upright in the unfamiliar bed, heart hammering. The cheap hotel clock on the nightstand glowed *05:01 AM.*

Then came the voice—deep, gravelly, like someone had been gargling asphalt and whiskey for breakfast since '92.

"ON YOUR FEET, CANDYASS! YOU'VE GOT TEN SECONDS TO OPEN THIS DOOR OR I'M COMING THROUGH IT."

Afsar scrambled out of bed, feet slapping the tile floor as he lunged for the handle. He flung the door open just in time to be met with a wall of a man.

His instructor stood there, arms crossed over a massive chest. He wore a faded olive drab t-shirt tucked into cargo pants, boots already caked in desert dust. His skin was tanned leather, a roadmap of sun and scars, and his cropped salt-and-pepper hair did little to soften the storm in his eyes.

"You Afsar Ramos?" he barked.

"Yes, sir," Afsar said, voice still rough with sleep.

"Not *sir*. I work for a living. You can call me *Chief*. Chief Adams."

"Got it."

Chief pushed past him into the room without waiting for an invitation. He gave it a once-over with a scowl.

"Room's too clean. You sleep like a tourist?"

"I was told we started today," Afsar said carefully.

"You *started* the second you stepped off that plane, sweetheart," Chief growled. "You don't wait for the game to begin. You *are* the game."

He spun back around and shoved a small duffel bag into Afsar's chest.

"Put this on. You've got five minutes. Uniform's in there, boots included. Leave your pride behind and double-time it to the quad. You'll find it easy enough—just follow the sound of screaming."

Afsar clutched the bag, nodding.

Chief leaned in closer, his breath heavy with coffee and menace. "This isn't college. This isn't theory. This isn't for grades. You screw up out here, someone dies—maybe you. Maybe worse, me. Got it?"

Afsar met his gaze. "Got it."

Chief narrowed his eyes, nodded once, then turned on his heel and stalked out. Afsar shut the door behind him and exhaled.

He dropped the duffel on the bed and unzipped it. Inside were a set of durable tactical fatigues, boots, and a plain name patch: *RAMOS*.

As he began changing, the sun barely creeping over the ridge outside, he muttered to himself under his breath.

"Welcome to the deep end."

The quad was a brutal stretch of dirt and gravel hemmed in by low buildings and a wire fence topped with concertina. The rising sun turned the Nevada dust into gold, but there was nothing warm about the place.

Afsar jogged into the open yard, breath short, boots thudding against the hardpack, sweat already clinging to his shirt.

Chief Adams stood in the center of the space, arms crossed, eyes like steel traps waiting to snap shut.

"Five minutes?" Chief barked as Afsar came to a halt. "*Five* minutes means you're late, Ramos! Around here, when I say five, you show in *three*. You wanna survive this course, you better start subtracting your damn minutes."

"Yes, Chief," Afsar said, standing at attention, trying not to wince from the stitch in his side.

Chief stepped toward him, close enough that Afsar could see the constellation of scars on his forearms. His voice dropped a register—calmer, but heavier.

"This is not a summer camp. This is not boot camp. This is *Selection*. You were picked because someone somewhere thinks you have potential. I'm here to prove them right… or bury that fantasy in the desert."

He turned and pointed to a long steel structure near the edge of the quad—an obstacle course that looked like it was designed by a sadist with a grudge against the human body.

"For the next three weeks, you will be broken down—physically, mentally, emotionally. You will eat, sleep, and breathe discomfort. You will do things that your body tells you it *can't* do, and then you'll do more. Because if you can't do more, someone dies."

Chief's voice carried across the quad now, directed at the few other recruits trickling into formation.

"You will learn evasive driving, firearms proficiency, hand-to-hand combat, wilderness survival, interrogation resistance, urban surveillance, and cultural submersion. You'll be taught how to fight, how to vanish, how to kill, and—more importantly— when *not* to."

He turned back to Afsar, eyes narrowing.

"You screw up, Ramos, I don't yell—I just write you off. You don't want to be written off."

"I won't screw up," Afsar said, jaw set.

"We'll see," Chief replied.

A long silence passed between them before Chief nodded toward the course.

"Warm-up starts there. First lap's just to see if you puke. Second lap's to see if you faint. Third lap's to see if you actually belong here."

Then he blew a sharp whistle and barked, "GO!"

Afsar took off running—heart pounding, lungs already burning—and behind him, Chief's voice rang out like thunder:

"THREE MINUTES MEANS READY TO FIGHT, RAMOS. LET'S SEE IF YOU'RE A FIGHTER OR A FANTASY!"

Afsar's chest heaved as he cleared the final wall on his third lap through the obstacle course. His palms were scraped, his shirt soaked through with sweat, and his legs trembled from the strain. He dropped to his knees at the end, dust clinging to his skin like war paint.

Chief Adams stood over him, clipboard in hand, impassive behind a pair of mirrored sunglasses.

"Not the worst I've seen," Chief muttered, marking something down. "Not the best either. But you didn't quit. That counts."

Afsar looked up, sucking in a breath. "I'll be better tomorrow."

Chief cracked the faintest hint of a smile. "You'd better be."

He glanced over his shoulder, as if checking the wind—or the presence of invisible ears—then turned back to Afsar, serious again.

"Now listen up," he said, squatting down so they were eye-level. "You're on a joint-use base, Ramos. The CIA runs this corner, but there are other agencies here—some with stripes, some without. You'll see hangars, buildings, fences, even airstrips that you're *not* cleared for. Don't ask questions. Don't wander. Don't even *look* too long."

Afsar nodded, still catching his breath.

"If you're caught past a red line, or in a building that's not yours to be in, you don't get a warning. You get escorted off the property, badge revoked, future in flames. That's not a threat. It's the policy. Understood?"

"Yes, Chief. Understood."

Chief stood, towering again. "Good. You're dismissed for breakfast. Mess hall's that way— building with the flag and the faded Coke machine out front. You've got twenty minutes, then you report to Ops Room Bravo for your briefing."

Afsar staggered to his feet, legs aching but pride swelling just a bit.

"Oh, and Ramos," Chief said as Afsar turned to go.

"Yes, Chief?"

"That wasn't bad for a first run. But if you want to last here, you better train like someone's trying to kill you—because one day, someone will."

Afsar swallowed and gave a sharp nod. "Roger that."

Then he limped off toward the mess hall, heart pounding—not just from exertion anymore, but from the weight of where he was… and what he was becoming.

The sun had just begun to rise over the jagged Nevada mountains, casting long shadows across the compound as the sound of boots hitting dirt echoed through the desert basin. Afsar moved in perfect rhythm with the others in his cohort, sweat darkening the gray of his shirt, his breath steady despite the pace. Five miles every morning. No exceptions.

"Pick up those knees, Ramos!" Chief bellowed from a dusty trail ridge, arms folded across his chest like a sentry carved from rock.

"Yes, Chief!" Afsar shouted, pushing harder.

The air was dry and thin, but after years training in Tennessee's wet, suffocating summers, this heat didn't feel like death. It felt like a crucible—hot enough to burn away weakness, but clean, almost sterile. His body was adapting fast.

Later that morning, as they returned from the run, Afsar jogged beside Reyes, another recruit from the East Coast.

"Thought you said you hated the desert," Reyes panted, slapping dust off his shorts.

"I did," Afsar replied, grinning through the sweat. "Turns out I just hate bugs."

Reyes laughed. "Fair enough."

By the second week, Chief upped the ante. Every afternoon, they loaded into battered Humvees and drove north into the mountains—high desert, sharp switchbacks, punishing inclines. The packs were weighted. The pace was brutal.

"Footing is everything!" Chief barked as the group started their first hike. "Lose your step here, you don't sprain an ankle—you shatter it. And then you're done. No glory in being a liability."

The trail wove up through rocky canyons and loose shale slopes. Afsar led the back half of the group, careful, calculating. The air grew thinner as they climbed, but he liked the rhythm of it—step, balance, breathe. His legs burned, but not in the same way as those first days. It was a burn he welcomed now. A sign of progress.

Each evening, they returned blistered and dusty, collapsing into the benches at the mess hall, where lukewarm food tasted like heaven. Between spoonfuls of instant mashed potatoes and protein-heavy stew, conversation buzzed low around the room.

"You ever done anything like this before?" a recruit named Dev asked him one night.

"No," Afsar replied, wiping sweat from his brow. "But I've had people in my life who trained me for moments like this."

Dev raised a brow. "Military family?"

Afsar hesitated, then nodded once. "Something like that."

Chief walked past their table, catching the tail end of the conversation. "No one cares what you were before," he said without breaking stride. "Only what you are now—and what you'll survive long enough to become."

Afsar didn't say anything. He just kept eating, jaw set, eyes clear. Every drop of sweat, every aching muscle, every hard mile—it was all earning him a future. One grueling day at a time.

The door creaked open just before dawn. No barking orders this time. No booming voice. Just the sound of boots scuffing against the concrete floor.

Afsar stirred, squinting through the dim light as Chief stood in the doorway, expression unreadable.

"Up," Chief said quietly.

Afsar sat upright, confused. "What time is it?"

Chief didn't answer. Instead, he tossed a black cloth onto the bed.

"Put that on. Over your eyes."

Afsar hesitated only a moment. He slipped the blindfold over his head, tying it snugly behind him.

Chief's hand clapped down on his shoulder. "Good. Don't speak unless I tell you to."

The next sounds were mechanical: a door shutting, locks sliding, boots pacing. Afsar was guided out, one hand on his shoulder and another steering him forward by the elbow. He could feel the chill of early desert morning on his skin, even through his shirt.

He was loaded into what felt like a Jeep or Humvee— the suspension stiff, the engine rough and loud. He sat in the back, the road beneath him rough and winding. The ride stretched endlessly, twisting turns, sudden stops and starts. There was no telling where they were going. That was the point.

Time slowed, warped. All Afsar could do was count the bumps in the road, try to remember the angles of the turns—but even that became a blur after the first twenty minutes.

Eventually, the vehicle slowed, then stopped. Gravel crunched under tires. A door opened.

A firm hand gripped his arm and helped him out. Two sets of boots walked beside him. Then one stopped. The other led him a few more paces down what felt like a dirt trail.

Then, nothing.

Silence.

The sound of the vehicle driving away.

Wind brushing over dry desert.

And then a voice—disembodied, calm but sharp— spoke from behind him.

"Count to five hundred. Then take off the blindfold. Good luck."

Afsar turned his head instinctively, but there was nothing. No footfalls. No echo. Just the hush of the desert.

He exhaled slowly, centered himself, and began to count aloud.

"One... two... three..."

Each number sharpened his focus. The chill air was beginning to warm as the sun rose over the horizon. Sand shifted beneath his boots. A faint metallic clink—something had been left behind beside him.

"...four hundred ninety-eight... four hundred ninety-nine... five hundred."

He slipped the blindfold off.

The world snapped into focus. Pale morning sunlight cut across a dusty ridge, casting long shadows. Nothing but open desert as far as the eye could see—sparse scrub, rock formations, no trail, no structures.

At his feet sat a single weathered backpack.

Afsar crouched, unzipping it. Inside: a compass, a laminated map with no landmarks except a red X on the far corner, a ration bar, one full canteen, two purification tablets, a roll of gauze, a knife, and a hand-written note:

"You have 48 hours. Use what you've got. Make it back to base."

He looked around one more time. No one in sight. No tire tracks. Just sun, sand, and silence.

Afsar studied the map that he had been given a little close and noticed a much smaller X on the map. The area around the black X on the map was mountainous are rugged. The area around the bigger red X was flat and isolated. The area around the red X looked like the terrain around the base in his opinion, so he decided to use the compass to start heading in the direction of the red X from the approximate location of the smaller black X.

He tightened the straps of the pack, drew a deep breath, and took his first step.

For nearly two days, Afsar moved through the unforgiving desert like a ghost—deliberate, methodical, driven. The sun beat down during the day, searing the back of his neck and pulling every ounce of moisture from his body. At night, the cold snapped against his skin, and every shadow looked like a threat.

He rationed his water with precision, treated a nasty blister with the gauze by the end of the first day, and used the stars to navigate when the compass readings felt unreliable. More than once, he thought he heard movement—an animal, maybe, or someone watching him. But he kept going. Always forward.

On the second morning, his legs were jelly. His calves screamed, his lips were cracked, and his head pounded from the heat and lack of sleep. As his progress was starting to pick up on that second morning, he heard a low growl to his left. He looked over to see a coyote laying under a thiselbrush staring at him. He grabbed the K-bar knife that had been provided him out of his bag and turned to face the predator looking for his next meal. The standoff lasted for about five minutes, but seemingly feeling like hours before the animal got bored and turned in the opposite direction and slowly fled the scene. Afsar watched him go until the animal was just a faint dot on the horizon, then turned to continue on his way. He was close—he could feel it in his bones.

He crested a hill in the fading afternoon light and froze. In the distance, just beyond a rust-colored ridge, was the high, flat silhouette of the base. It might as well have been heaven.

He stumbled the last mile, more on instinct than strength, heart hammering as the sun dipped toward the horizon.

When he reached the outer gate with four hours still on the clock, he collapsed to his knees and let out a shaky breath.

Chief was waiting for him, arms folded, leaning against the fence like he'd been there all day. A faint, crooked grin pulled at the edge of his sun-creased face.

"Well, I'll be damned," he said, straightening up. "You actually made it."

Afsar looked up, chest heaving, eyes bloodshot but steady. "I told you I would."

Chief chuckled, slow and gravelly. "Plenty talk a big game. Most wash out halfway through Day One."

Afsar forced himself to his feet, shoulders squared despite the trembling in his legs. "You said make it back. So I did."

Chief's grin widened just a notch. He nodded, impressed, then gestured toward the compound.

"Not bad," he said. "Now the real training begins."

He turned and started walking. Afsar followed, each step heavy but sure. There was no turning back now.

Chief slowed his pace as they neared the barracks, his boots crunching against the gravel. The late-day sun painted everything in long, golden shadows. Afsar's legs still ached, but his mind was already surging forward—he had passed the test, but the way Chief said "real training" had weight. Layers. Consequences.

As they reached the steps, Chief stopped and turned to face him, the grin gone, replaced with something harder, more deliberate.

"You did alright out there," he said, tone flat but not unkind. "But survival in the desert's one thing. Blending in halfway across the world's another."

Afsar nodded, wiping the sweat from his brow.

"So what's next?"

Chief's eyes narrowed slightly, like he was measuring something in Afsar again. Then he answered:

"Cultural and language training starts Monday. Bright and early. You're gonna learn how to move, speak, and think like the people we work among. Mistakes out there don't get second chances."

Afsar met his gaze without flinching. "I understand."

Chief gave a final nod. "Rest up, rookie. You've earned it. But Monday? That's when it gets real."

He turned and disappeared into the main building, leaving Afsar alone with the setting sun, the ache in his muscles, and the steady drumbeat of purpose building in his chest.

He had made it this far. Monday couldn't come soon enough.

***

2011

The Saturday sun had barely peeked over the rooftops, but Afsar was already awake, stuffing his backpack with gear he had triple-checked the night before—mess kit, flashlight, compass, extra socks. His room looked like a miniature base camp. The Scout handbook lay open on his desk, its pages worn and creased.

Downstairs, the front door creaked open and then slammed shut.

"Afsar!" came the voice of his best friend, Brian, practically bursting with energy. "You ready yet, or what?"

Afsar zipped up his pack and slung it over his shoulder, bounding down the stairs with a rare grin stretched across his face.

"I've been ready since Tuesday," he said, adjusting the brim of his cap.

Brian grinned. "Same. I've been dreaming about the obstacle course. And the giant campfire. And the chili cookoff! My dad says we're gonna win this year."

"You always say that" Afsar replied, elbowing him playfully as they stepped out onto the porch. "Last year, you burned the beans."

"That was a *smoky flavor profile,* thank you very much," Brian said, puffing out his chest in mock pride.

Afsar laughed—really laughed—and the sound was like a breeze pushing aside months of quiet. It had been a hard year. The hardest. Since his Mom passed, there were days when it felt like the world had gone dull and flat. But lately, trivial things—like Scout meetings, the smell of pine sap, and the way Brian could still make him laugh—had started to bring color back in.

Jack, Afsar's dad, came out to the porch, car keys in hand.

"You two mountain men ready?" he asked, scanning the boys' packs. "You've got your canteens? First-aid kit?"

"Yes, sir," Afsar answered. "Double-checked."

Jack ruffled his son's hair before unlocking the car. "Alright then. Let's hit the road. Jamboree waits for no one."

As the boys piled into the backseat, Brian whispered, "This year's gonna be the best one yet."

Afsar nodded, eyes steady as he looked out the window.

"Yeah," he said. "I think it will be."

The last night of the Jamboree crackled with the sound of firewood and laughter. Scouts from across the state had gathered around the massive campfire, trading patches, telling stories, roasting marshmallows until they were golden brown—or black, depending on the kid's skill level.

Afsar sat beside Brian, legs stretched out, face lit by the orange glow. The stars above were a glittering ocean, and the mountain air had just the right kind of chill. For the first time in what felt like forever, Afsar felt normal.

Brian nudged him with an elbow. "Hey," he whispered, eyes gleaming, "you ever been on a snipe hunt?"

Afsar gave him a side-eyed look. "A snipe hunt? That's not even real, man."

Brian grinned mischievously. "Exactly. But *they* don't know that." He nodded toward a group of younger scouts sitting nearby. "We'll make it look like we're going for something serious. You in?"

Afsar hesitated for half a second, then smirked. "I'm in."

They grabbed flashlights, a canvas sack, and announced to the younger scouts that they were headed out to catch the elusive snipe—an extremely rare, nocturnal bird, apparently best found near the creek bed just past the ridge. The younger scouts watched in awe as the two boys disappeared into the woods, playing it up for all it was worth.

But after twenty minutes of weaving through trees, following half-baked guesses and laughing themselves hoarse, the mood shifted.

"Wait," Brian said, shining his flashlight around. "Wasn't that fallen tree the one we passed an hour ago?"

"I thought we went left at the split?" Afsar asked, eyes narrowing. "No… we went right. I think."

The laughter stopped.

The woods suddenly felt darker. Every branch cracked louder, every gust of wind seemed sharper. Their flashlights flickered uncertainly.

They tried retracing their steps—but with every turn, it became clearer they were lost. Afsar checked his watch. Midnight had come and gone.

"Maybe we should just stop walking," Afsar said, voice tight. "If we keep going, we'll get even more turned around."

Brian nodded slowly. "Yeah… you're right."

They found a small clearing near a boulder and huddled together under their jackets, flashlights off to save battery. They didn't talk much after that—just listened to the forest, and the pounding of their own hearts.

Dawn crept in slowly.

Voices finally called through the trees.

"Afsar! Brian!"

"Over here!" they shouted, scrambling to their feet.

It was Jack—and two scoutmasters—looking equal parts relieved and furious.

As they were marched back toward camp, Jack shot Afsar a look that was somewhere between *you're grounded for life* and *thank God you're safe.*

"You went out looking for *snipe?*" Jack said in disbelief.

Brian tried to explain. "It was just supposed to be a joke—like, a camp tradition!"

Jack let out a long breath. "Next time, how about a joke that doesn't require search parties?"

Afsar nodded, sheepish but grinning faintly. "Yes, sir."

Later that morning, back at camp, Brian leaned over and whispered, "That... was *almost* worth it."

Afsar cracked a tired smile. "Almost."

Chapter 10

The training facility's language wing looked more like a university building than anything military—clean white walls, corkboards filled with regional maps and dialect charts, and shelves of textbooks worn at the corners from years of use. The overhead lights hummed quietly as Afsar took a seat near the front of the room. A handful of other recruits, most older than him, filtered in behind him, settling into their desks.

Chief stood at the front—not in fatigues this time, but khakis and a polo, clipboard in hand. He scanned the room with his usual half-scowl before speaking.

"Language and cultural immersion. The difference between blending in and getting caught. Between building trust and blowing a mission. Take it seriously."

Afsar sat up straighter.

Chief continued. "For the next eight weeks, you'll be working with native instructors in Dari, Farsi, and Pashto. You'll study customs, tribal affiliations, etiquette, and regional politics. This isn't about phrases—it's about understanding how people live and think. Got it?"

Murmurs of agreement rippled across the room.

Chief turned to a middle-aged Afghan man standing off to the side. "This is Mr. Sadat. He'll be your lead instructor. Treat him with respect. He speaks five languages better than most of you speak English."

Sadat gave a modest nod. "Salaam, bacheha. Welcome."

The session kicked off with introductions in Dari. Afsar's turn came, and he rose confidently to his feet.

"Salam, naamam Afsar ast. Man az Tennessee hastam, vali zaban-e Dari, Farsi, wa Pashto ra khoob midanam."
(Hello, my name is Afsar. I'm from Tennessee, but I know Dari, Farsi, and Pashto well.)

There was a brief pause in the room.

Sadat raised an eyebrow, impressed. "Khoob. Cheqadr waqti zaban yad gerefti?" (Good. How long have you studied the language?)

Afsar shrugged, grinning. "Mādar-am az Afghanistan bood. Man az oo az kuchiki yad gereftam." (My mother is from Afghanistan, I learned it from her when I was little.)

A few of the recruits gave him side glances, and Afsar sat down with a bit too much satisfaction.

Chief's eyes narrowed.

After the class ended, as the group gathered their notes, Chief called out, "Afsar. Hang back a second."

Afsar froze. "Yes, sir."

When the room emptied, Chief leaned against the desk, arms crossed. "Fluent in three languages. Impressive. But let me tell you something, kid—this isn't a spelling bee."

Afsar blinked. "Sir?"

"You want to impress people? Do it by listening more than talking. We're not here to crown you top student. We're here to mold you into something useful. Humility travels further than perfect grammar. Don't forget that."

Afsar's mouth pressed into a line. "Understood, sir."

Chief gave him a nod and turned back toward the door. "Get to the mess. You've got cultural protocols in twenty."

Afsar lingered a second longer, the sting of the rebuke settling behind his ribs. He wasn't sorry he knew the languages—but he was starting to understand: there was a difference between knowing something and proving you were ready to use it.

He grabbed his binder and headed down the hall—quieter now, more focused.

The desert heat had already started to bite when Afsar stepped into the shaded classroom trailer. Ceiling fans spun lazily overhead, offering little relief. He dropped his notebook onto the desk with a light thud and greeted the instructor in Dari without thinking.

"Subh bakhair, mo'allem. Chand so'al daram." (Good morning, teacher. I have a few questions.)

Mr. Kazemi, a former interpreter for the Special Forces and now a cultural advisor, gave him a sideways look. "You sure you're not from Kabul, kid?"

Afsar grinned. "Born and raised in Tennessee. Just listened more than I talked growing up."

Chief stood at the back of the room, arms folded, watching the interaction. After the first week of language immersion, it was clear to everyone—Afsar wasn't just competent. He was fluent, confident, and culturally intuitive in a way that usually took years of deployment to develop.

That afternoon, Chief called a meeting with the instructors.

"We're wasting time," Chief said, straight to the point, as always. "The kid's ahead of the pack."

Kazemi nodded. "He's not just speaking the language. He understands the subtleties—the tribal nuances, the historical context. I taught Marines who couldn't tell the difference between Pashto and Farsi after six months. He's quoting 14th-century Persian poets before lunch."

Chief scratched his chin. "I want to fast-track him. Push him to the advanced tier. Shadow ops prep. Simulations. Real-world case studies."

"He's young," another instructor offered, cautiously. "Barely out of college."

"And already sharper than half the veterans I've trained," Chief shot back. "Let's challenge him. See how high he can really climb."

—

The next morning, Afsar arrived to find the classroom nearly empty. Only Chief waited by the door.

"You're not in here anymore," Chief said. "You're heading to Building 9. Congratulations."

Afsar blinked. "Building 9? That's…"

"The simulation wing. Real-time immersion, case modeling, and deception training. You earned it." Chief paused, stepping closer. "But wipe that smug look off your face. You speak the languages, kid. Now it's time to prove you understand the people."

Afsar nodded, serious now. "Yes, sir."

As he walked away, Chief called after him.

"Oh—and don't embarrass us in front of the CIA brass. They'll be watching."

Afsar didn't turn around, but the corners of his mouth twitched into a smile.

Building 9 looked like every other structure on base—plain, beige, sun-bleached—but the keypad-locked doors and the camera perched on the corner of the roof made it clear it wasn't just another classroom.

Afsar swiped the temporary badge Chief had given him. A green light blinked, and the heavy steel door buzzed open.

Inside, the air conditioning blasted like a meat locker. Fluorescent lights hummed above as Afsar stepped into a corridor lined with unmarked doors. A tall woman in tactical black waited for him at the end, arms folded.

"You're Afsar," she said, voice crisp.

"Yes, ma'am."

"I'm Vaughn. I run this program. You impress me, you move up. You waste my time, you go back to Chief's drills until your boots wear out."

"Yes, ma'am," he said again, posture straightening instinctively.

She turned on her heel. "Follow."

They entered a room that looked like a tiny village—mud brick walls, rugs on the floor, hanging lanterns. Afsar blinked. The scents of cumin and old wood filled the space, piped in through hidden vents. He could hear voices speaking Pashto in another room.

"This is our sim suite," Vaughn explained. "You'll walk through scenarios pulled from real-world cases. Diplomatic tensions, tribal negotiations, intelligence retrieval. Sometimes you'll mediate. Sometimes you'll persuade. And sometimes you'll lie."

She stopped in front of a curtained doorway and pulled the curtain aside.

Inside sat a man in traditional Afghan dress, sipping tea cross-legged on the floor. Afsar's eyes narrowed. Something about the man's posture—relaxed but alert—told him this wasn't just a role-player.

"First test," Vaughn said, gesturing inside. "He's an elder. He's angry. He thinks the Americans insulted his family. You're the bridge."

Afsar nodded, took a breath, and stepped through the curtain.

The man looked up sharply. "To ba chand sal dari sohbat me-koni ke ba pesh-e man, sar baland me-ayi?"
(How many years have you spoken Dari that you come before me with your head held high?)

Afsar bowed respectfully and replied, "Az dokhtar-e madaram yad gereftam. Oo az Spera bood. Ba bozorgi shoma ertefa' nadaaram—faghat mekhaham fahmida shavad."
(I learned from my mother's side. She was from Spera. I don't claim to stand above your greatness—I only wish to understand.)

The man stared at him, then gave the faintest nod and gestured to sit.

From behind the one-way glass, Vaughn scribbled a note on her clipboard and murmured, "Let's see what else the kid's got."

Afsar lowered himself cross-legged across from the man, mimicking the elder's posture. He didn't speak immediately. He let the silence settle between them, the way his father once taught him—let the air fill with tension, then ease it with humility.

The elder finally broke the quiet. "They sent a child to speak for the Americans. Is this how little they value us now?"

Afsar looked him in the eyes, calm and steady. "It is because they value you that they sent someone who was taught respect before he was taught politics."

The man raised an eyebrow. "Words are easy. Respect is shown. Tell me—would your mother allow you to speak for her people?"

Afsar's jaw tightened, but he nodded. "She would tell me to listen before speaking. And to remember that pride without wisdom is just noise."

A pause.

"Hmm." The elder took another sip of tea, his expression unreadable. "You say your mother was from Khost. Do you remember her village?"

"Spera," Afsar answered without hesitation. "She used to describe the mountains like they were giants watching over her. She missed them every day."

The elder's face softened slightly, though his tone remained firm. "The Americans bombed a wedding near Spera last year. Children died. If you want my help, tell me—why should I trust you?"

Afsar exhaled slowly. This was the moment.

"You shouldn't," he said. "Not yet. Trust should be earned. But I'm here because I want to learn your story, not rewrite it."

The elder leaned back, eyes narrowing as he studied the young man before him. Then, almost imperceptibly, he nodded.

"Very well… we talk."

Behind the glass, Vaughn allowed herself a rare smile. She turned to the analyst beside her.

"Tell Chief: the kid's more than a quick study. He's a mirror. He gives them exactly what they need to see."

"Should we increase the scenario complexity?"

"Double it," Vaughn said, already reaching for the next folder. "Let's see if he holds up under pressure."

Afsar sat on the edge of the cold metal chair in the debriefing room, a plain white space with one wall of two-way glass and the faint hum of overhead fluorescents. His shirt clung to his back, damp with sweat he hadn't realized he was shedding until now. The door opened quietly, and Chief stepped in, a folder in one hand, a paper cup of coffee in the other.

Chief didn't sit. He stood across from Afsar, flipping open the folder with practiced ease. "You think that went well?"

Afsar blinked. "He agreed to talk. He opened up."

"That's not what I asked," Chief said, taking a slow sip. "I asked if *you* think it went well."

Afsar hesitated. "I kept my cool. I stuck to what I knew, related personally without pandering. I didn't push too hard."

Chief grunted. "You forgot to ask one critical question: what *he* wanted out of the conversation."

Afsar furrowed his brow. "He didn't seem open to negotiations yet—"

"That's not the point. People don't open up unless they see something in it for them. Information flows when they feel in control. You gave him sympathy, family connection… but not leverage. You have to make them think they've got a grip on the wheel, even when you're steering."

Afsar sat back slightly, absorbing the hit without flinching. "Understood."

Chief finally sat, placing the cup down. "You've got instincts, I'll give you that. Most recruits would've walked in trying to impress him with intel or credentials. You led with humility. That's rare."

Afsar looked up. "But?"

"But…" Chief leaned in, voice low and firm. "That humility better be armor, not an opening. These people aren't your friends. They're assets, informants, maybe threats. You can respect them. You can even learn from them. But never forget the role you're here to play."

Afsar's jaw tightened. "I know the role."

"Do you?" Chief asked. "Because Vaughn thinks you've got the potential for Tier One fieldwork. That means real-world placement. That means getting in, staying in, and getting out with your soul intact. It means knowing when to speak Dari like a native and when to shut your damn mouth."

Afsar gave a short nod. "Then I guess I've got more to learn."

Chief closed the folder. "Good answer. Because tomorrow, we're upping the stakes."

He stood and moved toward the door, then paused.

"Oh—and you passed."

Afsar blinked. "I passed?"

"Technically. Barely. Don't let it go to your head. You're still green."

As the door clicked shut behind Chief, Afsar let out a slow breath and glanced at the mirror. He knew they were still watching. Always watching.

He straightened his shoulders, jaw set.

The desert wind kicked up dust as Afsar jogged across the compound toward the training field, boots pounding the gravel in a steady rhythm. The sun was just breaching the horizon, casting a golden hue over the sand-colored buildings and long, silent fences. Another day of drills, fieldcraft, languages, and mind games. His body ached from the relentless pace, but his mind was sharp—sharper than it had ever been.

Except today felt… off.

As he reached the edge of the training field, Afsar slowed to a walk. The usual clang of weights and barked instructions were absent. Instead, Chief stood alone near the edge of the empty quad, arms crossed, sunglasses hiding his eyes.

Afsar approached cautiously. "Morning, Chief. What's the plan? More shadowing exercises or—"

"No plan." Chief interrupted, voice gravelly but calm. "Drop your pack, Afsar."

He blinked, unsure. "Sir?"

"I said drop it. Training's over."

Afsar hesitated, then slowly shrugged the rucksack off his shoulder and let it fall to the ground. "Over as in… a break?"

"Over as in *complete*," Chief replied flatly, then pulled a small envelope from his back pocket and handed it over. "You've got a message."

Afsar took it, heart rate ticking up. The envelope was plain white, unmarked. His name scrawled across it in tight, clean handwriting he recognized instantly.

Ambar.

He looked up at Chief, whose expression hadn't changed.

"She left it this morning," Chief said. "Told me to give it to you. And told me to tell you this: *'He's ready.'* That's all."

Afsar's fingers tightened around the envelope. "So that's it? No final review? No debrief?"

Chief shook his head once. "This was the review. You made it through. No red flags, no slips. You didn't just survive, you adapted. That's what we look for."

He paused, then added with a rare, faint trace of pride, "You didn't fold, even when we tried to break you. That counts for something."

Afsar looked down at the envelope again. "So what now?"

Chief glanced over his shoulder at the hangar-like building in the distance—Building Nine. Then back to Afsar.

"Now," he said, stepping aside, "you go where the message tells you. This is where the real work begins."

Afsar slid a finger under the flap of the envelope, hesitating just a second before opening it.

Afsar unfolded the note with steady hands, eyes scanning the clean script of Ambar's handwriting:

"Report to Building 9 immediately. Important briefing. – A."

No code. No riddles. Just direct. Urgent.

Without a word to Chief, Afsar nodded and turned on his heel, legs already moving across the compound. The Nevada sun was now fully up, casting long shadows across the gravel paths. His boots kicked up dust as he made the familiar trek, each step feeling heavier with the weight of what might be coming.

When he reached Building 9, the usual silence of the structure seemed to hum with tension. Inside, the debriefing room was dimly lit. A single television screen had been rolled into the center of the space—clearly not part of the usual setup.

He stepped in, the door clicking shut behind him.

The TV screen flickered to life.

Ambar, face drawn and eyes sharp behind glasses, filled the screen.

"Afsar, we've got a situation."

Afsar's body straightened instinctively.

"A UNAMA team—three workers, two British women and a Dutch national—have been kidnapped by an Al-Qaeda splinter cell in the Khost Province, near the village of Spera. The United Nations has requested CIA assistance."

Afsar's pulse quickened. The official leaned slightly forward.

"Your first field assignment begins now. You and your instructor will fly out tonight. Use your time en route to develop a rescue plan. Godspeed."

The screen went black.

Silence hung in the air for a single beat—long enough for Afsar to take one deep breath.

Then a voice behind him cut through the quiet.

Chief. No longer the drillmaster barking orders—this was something colder, sharper.

"Two hours," he said flatly. "Pack light. We move out."

Afsar turned and met his instructor's eyes. There was no ceremony, no handshake. Just purpose.

"Understood," Afsar said, voice low but steady.

By that evening, the sun had dipped behind the mountains, casting Las Vegas in a pink-orange glow as their flight lifted from the runway. The roar of the engines filled the silence between them as Afsar pored over maps, intelligence briefings, and reports with Chief beside him.

This wasn't simulation anymore.

***

2002

The sun baked the tarmac of Forward Operating Base Solereno, somewhere in southeastern Afghanistan, turning everything a shade of dusty gold. Inside the makeshift barracks, a tin-roofed structure that creaked when the wind blew too hard, Jack Ramos lounged back on a cot, boots off, dog tags clinking lightly as he thumbed through a worn-out paperback of *The Bourne Identity*.

"Ramos," Corporal Evans called out, tossing a deck of cards on the table as he leaned back. "How many times you read that book now?"

Jack grinned without looking up. "This'll be six. Maybe seven. You keep countin', Corporal, I might make you write the sequel."

The rest of the squad chuckled. The fan above buzzed loudly, stirring the stale heat but not relieving it. Outside, a Black Hawk thudded overhead, casting shadows across the red dirt.

Private First Class Dominguez popped his head in through the open door, sweat on his brow and a clipboard in hand.

"Jack, you're wanted in the CO's office," Dominguez said, a little breathless. "Now."

Jack raised an eyebrow and sat up, setting the book aside.

"Something wrong?" Evans asked.

"Don't know," Jack said, reaching for his boots. "But I doubt he called me in to chat about my reading habits."

He tugged on the laces, the motion practiced and quick. He stood, pulled on his camo shirt, and straightened the rank patch on his sleeve.

As he made his way across the compound, a couple of soldiers nodded in greeting, others too wrapped up in maintaining gear or prepping for patrol to notice. He passed the comms tent, the chow hall, and then stepped into the shadow of the command building.

Inside, it was slightly cooler. Lieutenant Colonel Hargrave's office was at the end of the corridor, guarded by a young MP who gave Jack a short nod and opened the door without a word.

Hargrave looked up from behind a battered wooden desk covered in maps, folders, and a steaming mug of coffee.

The flap of a side door opened quietly, and Jack's gaze shifted. Three men stepped into the room—bearded, weather-worn, and robed in traditional Afghan garments. Their faces were lined with age, but their posture was stiff with purpose. One of them, the oldest, wore a deep crimson turban and had a hawk-like glare. The two younger men flanked him, arms crossed and eyes flicking cautiously to Jack.

Colonel Hargrave cleared his throat. "Ramos, these are Gul Ahmad and his sons, Zahir and Rafiq. They're from the village of Spera, around the area of our last patrol. They say the girl you brought in—Afsoon—is their daughter and sister."

Jack's body tensed. His jaw tightened, and he slowly turned to face the men directly.

"The girl was terrified when we found her," Jack said evenly, not breaking eye contact with Hargrave. "She was barefoot, bleeding, running towards us. She told me she was running for her life. That her family planned to kill her because she was pregnant and unmarried."

The temperature in the room seemed to drop a few degrees.

The older man—Gul Ahmad—took a step forward, his face flushing red. He exploded, shouting in rapid-fire Dari. His voice cracked with fury, his finger jabbing toward Jack as the room filled with tension.

"Tu chi miguyee?! Ba dukhtaram tuheen mikuni?! Oo sharaf-e-khod ra kharab kard—oo az mard sharm namikeshad!"
("What are you saying?! You insult my daughter?! She disgraced her honor—she feels no shame before men!")

Jack stood up, voice low but firm. "I don't insult her. I protected her."

"She's a child," Jack continued, turning back to Hargrave. "A scared one. And if we hand her over, she'll be dead before sunset."

Zahir stepped forward now, his hands trembling as he spoke more measured than his father, though his tone was still cold. "This is not your country. You don't understand our customs."

"You're right," Jack replied. "But I know the difference between custom and murder."

Hargrave raised both hands, his expression flat but tight. "Enough. All of you."

The room fell into a taut silence, the only sound being the soft buzz of the overhead fluorescent light.

"Jack," Hargrave said, slowly and carefully, "step outside a moment."

Jack's eyes lingered on Gul Ahmad's for a moment longer before he gave a slow nod and backed toward the door. His pulse was rising. His gut told him this wasn't over.

As Jack stepped into the hallway, the door to Colonel Hargrave's office clicked shut behind him. His heart was still pounding from the confrontation, but he focused on steadying his breath. He leaned against the wall, eyes scanning the hall, though he was sure that

Gul Ahmad's fury and Zahir's cold stare were still burned into his mind.

A few minutes later, the door to the office opened again. Colonel Hargrave emerged first, his face an unreadable mask. The three men followed him in single file, their heads low but shoulders rigid, clearly still simmering with anger. The older man, Gul Ahmad, was muttering softly under his breath in Dari, clearly still seething, while his sons looked straight ahead, eyes hard.

Hargrave nodded to Jack, signaling for him to approach. "Ramos," he said, voice flat. "The men have been instructed to go to JAG and fill out the proper paperwork. We'll start the investigation. But given the seriousness of the accusations—and the fact that we don't have full context yet—the woman will remain in protective custody here on base until we can determine the truth of her story."

Jack nodded, not entirely satisfied but understanding the protocol. "Understood, sir."

As the three men moved to exit the building, Jack couldn't shake the feeling that things were far from over. Zahir was the last to pass by. He stopped just as he reached the door, and then slowly, deliberately, turned to face Jack. His cold, dead blue-eyed stare met Jack's, and for a moment, neither man moved. The hallway fell silent, the tension palpable.

Zahir's lips curled into a sneer, his voice low but icy. "Even if it takes my last breath," he spat, "I will find you, I will gut you like a dog, and I will restore my family's honor."

Jack's muscles tightened instinctively, but he didn't flinch. He just stood there, keeping his composure, refusing to show any sign of fear. Zahir's words hung in the air like a cold warning, but Jack wasn't about to back down. Not now.

The younger man didn't wait for a response. With a final glare, he turned and walked out the door, his footsteps echoing in the hallway as he disappeared down the corridor.

Colonel Hargrave's eyes narrowed at Jack, sensing the weight of what had just been said. "You heard that?"

"Yeah, sir. I heard it," Jack replied, his voice calm but there was a steel edge to it. "I'll keep my head on a swivel."

Hargrave nodded grimly, then turned to walk toward his office. "Just make sure you stay sharp, Jack. This thing isn't over."

Jack stayed where he was, his fists clenched at his sides, mentally preparing for the fallout. It wasn't the first time he'd heard threats from angry men—but there was something about Zahir's cold determination that made this one feel different. Dangerous.

And for the first time in a long while, Jack couldn't shake the feeling that trouble was just beginning to brew.

Chapter 11

The wheels of the Boeing 767 bumped against the runway of Kabul International Airport with a metallic groan, and the plane hissed as it taxied to a halt. The thick scent of dust, diesel, and distant wood smoke filtered in through the aircraft's ventilation system, triggering an odd cocktail of emotions in Afsar—anticipation, tension, purpose.

He followed Chief down the narrow gangplank, both of them lugging their compact travel gear, heads low against the bright Afghan morning sun. The hum of activity surrounded them: aid workers in neon vests, what passed for Afghan security forces in digital camo, UN vehicles weaving between hangars and terminals.

Chief didn't speak much as they moved toward the baggage claim area tucked in the back of a quiet terminal, away from the main passenger flow. He moved with the smooth confidence of a man who'd done this dozens of times. Afsar, by contrast, was alert, eyes scanning the room, soaking in every detail—the language, the uniforms, the gestures.

Their plain black duffels finally appeared on the slow-moving carousel. Chief grabbed his first, then hoisted

Afsar's off with one hand. From an outer pocket, he pulled a military-grade satellite phone wrapped in a protective rubber shell. He flipped the antenna up and punched in a series of numbers with the speed of muscle memory.

Afsar adjusted the strap on his shoulder and leaned closer. "Are we meeting someone here?"

Chief held up a finger, listening to the line ring. After a moment, someone picked up.

"This is Bravo-1-9. Package has arrived intact. Confirm rendezvous." A pause. "Copy that.."

He ended the call and turned to Afsar, tucking the phone back into his pack. "We've got a ride.. Civilian car. Local operative—don't talk unless spoken to."

Afsar nodded. "Got it."

Chief gave him a glance. "Don't look so eager. This ain't a tour. It gets real fast."

"I know," Afsar said quietly. "I'm ready."

Chief didn't reply right away. He just studied him for a beat, then turned toward the exit. "We'll see."

They pushed through the double glass doors into the arid Kabul air, the mountains rising like jagged ghosts in the distance. The noise, the smells, the unfamiliar rhythm of a city still healing from war—all of it hit Afsar at once.

The sun beat down hard as Afsar and Chief stepped out of the airport's grimy glass doors. Before the heat could fully settle into Afsar's skin, a dusty late-'90s Toyota Corolla rolled to a slow stop about twenty yards ahead of them, its headlights flashing twice.

"There's our guy," Chief muttered, adjusting his bag over one shoulder. "Let's go."

The car's faded white paint was streaked with desert grime, and the rear bumper was held up by zip ties. As they approached, the window rolled down with a wheeze, revealing a weathered face behind mirrored aviators and a cigarette dancing at the corner of a smirk.

"Which one of you fine gentlemen is the muscle, and which one's the brains?" the man said, voice raspy like gravel in a tin can. "Name's Walter. But everyone calls me Cran."

Chief opened the passenger door and motioned for Afsar to take the back seat.

"Cran?" Afsar asked, climbing in.

"Short for Cranston," the man said, putting the car into gear. "Bryan Cranston. Breaking Bad, my friend. Best damn show ever made. I've seen it through, I dunno, maybe twelve times. The way Walt ran that empire? Masterpiece. Genius. Brutal. Practical."

Afsar raised an eyebrow in the rearview. "That's… reassuring."

Chief grunted. "Just drive, Cran."

Cran took a long drag off his cigarette, blew the smoke out the side window, then merged into Kabul traffic like he'd done it a thousand times—which he probably had.

"You two must be the new ghosts in town," Cran said. "Not many Americans rolling through these. I assume whatever you're here for ain't tourism."

"Assume less," Chief said flatly, eyes scanning the road ahead.

Cran chuckled. "Alright, alright. I don't ask questions. I just drive. But fair warning—this city? She remembers everything. Smiles on the outside, bleeding on the inside."

The Corolla swerved around a donkey cart and zipped past a checkpoint with nothing more than a nod.

"Welcome to Kabul, boys," Cran muttered, tapping the ash from his cigarette into an empty bottle wedged in the console. "Let's see what kind of trouble we can avoid today."

Afsar watched the city slide by—its walls chipped from war, its people moving with wary purpose, its streets alive with tension and grit.

Cran glanced into the rearview mirror as the Corolla bounced over a pothole the size of a tire.

"Blending in is the key to survival here," he said, flicking the end of his cigarette into the wind. "But hell, son, you look like you grew up here. You'll do fine."

Afsar gave a small nod, his eyes taking in every alley, every storefront, every man with a Kalash slung casually over his shoulder. He didn't need to be told how close the edge was—they were driving on it.

The car weaved through Kabul's dense, chaotic sprawl for the better part of 45 minutes. Traffic here didn't follow rules so much as suggestions. Pedestrians darted across intersections. Trucks overloaded with watermelons swayed like drunk elephants. Horns blared in every direction, but no one seemed to care.

Eventually, the roads narrowed, then turned to uneven gravel and dirt. They passed a burned-out Soviet tank left to rust behind a barbed-wire fence before pulling into a dead-end alleyway. At the very end stood a structure that looked more like a junkyard sculpture than a building—corrugated tin sheets, broken cinderblocks, rusted nails sticking out at odd angles.

"Home sweet home," Cran muttered as he killed the engine.

He stepped out and tugged at a sagging piece of metal that served as a garage door. It screeched in protest but eventually folded upward like a hinge made of misery. He motioned for Chief to pull the car in.

Chief maneuvered the Corolla into the cramped space while Afsar climbed out, ducking under a low-hanging beam that threatened to scalp the unaware.

Cran let the garage door clatter back down behind them and locked it with what looked like a repurposed bicycle chain.

"It ain't the Ritz," Cran said, dusting off his hands, "but nobody looks twice at a place like this. That's the point."

Chief gave Afsar a look. "Welcome to fieldwork. You eat, sleep, and breathe out of holes like this now."

Afsar gave a wry smile. "As long as it's not leaking, I'll survive."

Cran chuckled as he pushed open the warped wooden door leading into the shack's dim interior. "Oh, it leaks, kid. But only when it rains… or when someone shoots at us. Either way, you'll get used to it."

The smell of dust, oil, and cheap incense hit Afsar's nose as they stepped inside. It was cramped, but functional—three cots, a table, an electronics setup that would be every teenage nerds dream, and a stack of dusty crates stamped with faded military codes.

Chief dropped his duffel on the nearest cot. "Get some rest. We'll review intel in a few hours."

Afsar nodded, silently taking in the room.

Cran clapped his hands once, the sound sharp and hollow in the tight space. "Alright, gentlemen," he said, sweeping his arm in a wide arc like he was unveiling a five-star resort, "welcome to the Solarium."

Chief raised an eyebrow. Afsar just waited.

Cran pointed to the left corner of the shack. "First stop on our grand tour: the kitchen."

What he was pointing at could barely claim the title. A warped, splintered plywood countertop sat on two mismatched cinder blocks. An old mini-fridge buzzed weakly beside it, its white paint stained yellow around the edges. On top, a dented electric kettle blinked like it hadn't worked since the Clinton administration. In the corner sat a teetering cardboard box filled with MREs, some of them clearly from the Gulf War.

Cran popped open the fridge, revealing three cans of beer and what might've once been cheese. "We got warm beer, salty rations, and a prayer or two if you're into that. Knock yourself out, gentlemen."

Chief leaned in, peering inside. "You could've led with the MREs. Beer looks like it fought in the Soviet withdrawal."

Afsar chuckled. "At least we know the fridge has a personality."

"Don't insult him," Cran said, shutting the fridge with a grunt. "He's sensitive."

Chief shook his head and dropped into the nearest chair, the metal legs groaning under the weight. "How long have you been holed up here, Cran?"

Cran grinned. "Too long. Long enough to name the fridge, short enough to still know how to make coffee that doesn't taste like diesel." He slapped the top of the kettle proudly. "She still works if you give her a good smack on the side and hold the plug in just right."

Afsar eyed the countertop. "I take it takeout isn't an option?"

Cran let out a laugh that rattled in his chest. "Oh sure, if you like your kebab with a side of hepatitis and bullets."

Chief smirked. "MREs it is, then."

Cran gave a small bow. "Five-star service."

He reached into the MRE box and tossed a pouch each to Chief and Afsar. "Dinner of champions. Don't say I never did nothin' for ya."

After dinner—which amounted to lukewarm chili mac, dry crackers, and a questionable chocolate bar—Cran dragged over a dented ammo crate and flipped it into a makeshift table. He unrolled a large, worn map onto the dust-caked floor, the edges curling with age. Afsar and Chief moved in, kneeling on either side as Cran smoothed it out with calloused hands.

"Khost Province," Cran muttered, tapping a finger near the eastern border. "This here's the village of Spera. Last confirmed location of the UNAMA team, according to Bar's intel."

Afsar leaned in, eyes scanning the terrain lines. "No solid confirmation of where they were taken after that?"

Cran shook his head. "Negative. We've got reports of movement south into the forested areas—maybe toward the border. This splinter group's slippery, doesn't play by usual patterns."

Chief narrowed his eyes. "Same map we saw in D.C."

"Pretty much," Cran grunted. "No fresh satellite pass, no drone footage. But we're expecting more intel by morning. Bar's people are supposed to push updated coordinates from Langley. Maybe even some SIGINT if the spooks get lucky."

Afsar glanced up. "We going in blind?"

Cran snorted. "Not blind. Just half-blind and underfed. But we'll fix that in the morning."

He folded the map back up, dusted off his hands, and stood. "Get some sleep, both of you. You're gonna need it."

Chief rose first. "Where's the luxury suite?"

Cran jerked a thumb toward a small side room, where two cots waited under a flickering bare bulb. "Room service ends at dusk."

Afsar offered a tired smile. "I'll take what I can get."

Cran gave them a curt nod. "Welcome to the job, boys." Then he turned away, the map tucked under his arm, leaving them to the silence of a Kabul night.

Chapter 12

The first rays of sunlight slipped through the cracks in the corrugated tin walls, casting golden slats across the dusty floor. Afsar stirred on the stiff cot, the thin blanket tangled around his legs, the sounds of Kabul beginning to stir outside—the distant bleat of goats, the sputtering of a motorcycle, a man calling out in Dari as he opened his small shop.

He sat up slowly, rubbing the sleep from his eyes. The air inside the shack was already warming up, dry and heavy with dust. He swung his legs over the side of the cot and pulled on his boots.

Chief's cot was empty. The faint smell of burned instant coffee drifted from the other room.

Afsar stepped into the kitchen—or what passed for one. Chief was leaning against the counter, sipping from a chipped enamel mug, eyes fixed on something outside through the slats in the metal wall.

"Mornin'," Afsar mumbled.

Chief didn't look over. "Sleep while you could, rookie. It doesn't get easier from here."

Afsar scratched his jaw and reached for an MRE. "Something cooking?"

"Cran is stirring something up," Chief said. "Cran's out back. Said he heard from Langley. Intel packet came through."

Afsar's brow lifted as he put the MRE back where he got it. "That fast?"

"Clock's ticking," Chief replied. "You've got ten minutes to eat and get your head on straight once Cran is done."

Cran pushed open the back door with his shoulder, the tin hinges squealing. His dusty boots thudded across the warped floor as he came in, grinning beneath his grizzled beard.

"Well, gentlemen," he said, tossing his satellite phone onto the table, "you're in luck."

Afsar glanced up. "That right?"

"Oh yeah," Cran said, wiping sweat from his brow with a faded rag. "Managed to scrounge up a special treat for you two. Don't say I never gave you anything."

Chief looked up from his mug, one brow cocked. "The last time someone said that to me, I spent four days on the toilet."

Cran chuckled. "You wound me, Chief. I'll have you know this one didn't come from a crate marked 'Do Not Consume After 1987.' This is fresh. Well… fresh-ish."

Afsar leaned forward slightly. "What is it?"

Cran held up a finger. "Patience, my friend. I like the suspense. Builds character." He turned and headed toward a beat-up cooler in the corner, whistling to himself.

Chief muttered, "If it moves, I'm shooting it."

Cran crouched beside the battered blue cooler, flipping the lid open with a little flair. A puff of cold air escaped into the warm room. He looked up at Afsar and Chief with a proud, toothy grin.

"Feast your eyes, boys. We're talking eggs stewed in tomato sauce, warm tandoori bread—straight off the griddle—spicy samosas, and a pot of proper milky chai. Cardamom and all."

Chief blinked. "You get all that in this dump?"

Cran pointed a finger at him. "This dump, my friend, has its secrets. You just gotta know who to bribe."

Afsar's eyes widened, a slow smile spreading across his face. "No way. That's what my mother used to make. Same smells, same spices. I haven't had food like that since…" His voice trailed off, but the warmth in his expression remained. "I'll devour my plate in ten minutes flat."

"Good," Cran said, standing and closing the cooler. "Because I'm not making it twice."

He stretched, groaned, and pointed a thumb toward the back door. "Gimme fifteen minutes to fire up the stove and burn a few knuckles. You'll be eating like warlords."

Afsar chuckled. "Take your time, Cran. Just knowing it's coming is enough."

Cran gave a satisfied nod and disappeared through the back door again, whistling a familiar tune under his breath—the faint rhythm of a man who found small joy in doing something right.

The smell of simmering tomatoes, spices, and freshly baked bread filled the shack, chasing away the morning chill. Cran returned with a tray balanced expertly on one calloused hand, setting it down on the wobbly table fashioned from old crates.

"Gentlemen," he said, placing plates in front of each of them. "Your five-star breakfast, courtesy of Chez Cran."

Afsar wasted no time. He scooped up a chunk of tandoori bread, dipped it into the rich tomato stew, and took a bite. His eyes closed for a moment. "God... this tastes like home."

Chief nodded as he chewed. "Not bad for a busted-up hideout in the middle of Kabul."

Cran grinned as he sat down with his own plate. "Told you. Good food's half the fight out here. That, and not getting your ass shot."

Afsar reached for a samosa. "Where'd you even find samosas this good?"

"Let's just say I have friends in low places," Cran replied, sipping his steaming cup of chai. "Some of 'em owe me favors. Some of 'em just like the color of American dollars."

Chief snorted. "More like the smell of 'em."

They ate in comfortable silence for a few minutes, save for the occasional appreciative hum or the thump of bread being torn apart. After finishing the last of his chai, Chief leaned back and glanced at the map still spread across the floor from the night before.

"Well," he said, wiping his mouth with his sleeve, "that was the calm. Time for the storm."

Cran nodded, licking a bit of tomato sauce from his thumb. "Yup. Time to earn your stripes, Afsar. Let's get to it."

Afsar grabbed the empty plates and stacked them neatly, brushing off the crumbs and wiping down the old wooden surface with a frayed rag. Chief folded the map and moved it aside while Cran slid a dented laptop from an ammo crate and powered it on, the fan wheezing like an asthmatic smoker.

"Alright," Cran said, his tone shifting from casual to businesslike. "Time to get our heads in the game."

Chief connected a portable hard drive to the laptop and nodded to Afsar. "Langley sent an updated packet. Just came in this morning. First thing we're looking at is the video that aired on Al-Maseerah and a couple fringe Arabic satellite channels."

Cran tapped a few keys, pulled the video file up, and rotated the laptop so they could all see. He clicked play.

The screen flickered to life, showing the three hostages seated on a patterned rug—two women, both British, and a Dutch man. They looked pale, exhausted, and clearly terrified. A masked man stood behind them, holding an AK-variant. His voice was sharp, deliberate, and filled with venom.

Afsar translated in a faint voice: "We are the Soldiers of the Right Path. The infidels you see before you were taken near Spera, in Khost. They have been judged. Their governments have seven days to pay ten million U.S. dollars. If they do not…"

The man unsheathed a long knife and held it above one of the women's heads.

"…they die."

The screen cut to black.

"Jesus," Chief muttered. "They've got no time to waste."

Cran leaned forward, arms on the table. "No masks we can match through facial rec but check the rug and the lantern in the corner. That's local. Khost, no doubt about it. Tribal patterns match the region. Probably within a ten-mile radius of Spera."

Afsar frowned. "They're feeding the video through a static relay. No metadata to trace. But the dialect? Khosti Pashto. Very specific. One of the men in the background used a phrase common among the Sabari district elders. Narrow enough?"

Chief gave him a slow nod. "It's a start. Let's cross-reference that with past SIGINT in the area. Cran, you've got that mesh-net surveillance file from three weeks ago?"

"Yeah," Cran said, already digging through a nearby folder. "Let me pull it. We might be able to triangulate chatter around the time they disappeared."

Cran flipped open another worn folder and tossed a handful of grainy satellite images onto the table. "Alright, here's what we've got from last week's flyover. These were pulled from the predator drone sweep after the UN flagged the kidnappings. Not much but look here—" he pointed to a cluster of mud-brick compounds on the outskirts of Spera, "—this one's got two armed sentries posted in broad daylight. That's not normal for a family dwelling."

Chief leaned in, squinting at the photo. "High walls, narrow entry point... good place to keep prisoners."

Afsar sifted through the other images, spreading them out. "This one," he said, tapping another compound in the village center, "was flagged by local HUMINT. A shopkeeper told one of our guys that outsiders were seen unloading crates here a few nights ago—crates, plural. Could be weapons or supplies for extended confinement."

Cran nodded, pulling a notepad from his pocket and jotting the grid coordinates. "That lines up with the cellphone intercepts we got from Langley. A burner pinged near this quadrant for thirteen minutes before dropping off completely."

Chief rubbed his jaw. "That's two possibles. What about the road to the east? Anything pop?"

"Yeah," Afsar said, reaching into the folder and sliding out a printed transcript. "A walk-in source reported seeing a dark Hilux drive out to this compound around the same time as the abduction. Same license plate pattern we flagged a month ago in connection with an Al-Qaeda courier cell."

"Three leads," Chief said, tapping his knuckles on the table. "But we need a fourth to cross-reference movement patterns. Something to help us rule out the noise."

Cran held up a hand. "Actually—wait. Last night, a UAV caught heat signatures moving into this ravine compound right before curfew. No cattle, no family signs. Just armed men. Thermal shows them staying put. No females detected... but they could be underground. It's been used as a safe house before."

Afsar nodded slowly. "Four targets. All viable. We'll need eyes on all of them before we can move."

Chief leaned back in his chair, exhaling. "Then we start tonight. We go in quiet. See what these ghosts are hiding." He looked at both men, eyes hard. "This mission doesn't get a second shot."

Cran folded his arms over his chest, expression grim. "One man gets in clean, makes the read, gets out quiet. Too many of us sniffing around that village and we light up like a bonfire in the middle of the desert."

Chief nodded. "And Afsar's the only one of us who can walk through that town without raising eyebrows. He knows the language, the customs, the rhythms. Hell, he could pass for someone's cousin coming home from the city."

Afsar looked between them. "You're both sure about this?"

Cran grunted. "You said you wanted the real thing, kid. This is it. Passive recon. No engagement, no hero plays. Eyes open, mouth shut."

Chief leaned forward, his voice low but firm. "You go in through Ghazni, take the old trade road south into Khost. We've decided that you will take the Corolla to the village outskirts. No mess, no questions."

Afsar nodded. "How long do I have?"

"Two nights," Chief replied. "Sunset on day two, you get out of there through the old shepherd's outpost north of the village. We'll be waiting with gear and plans back here, depending on what you find."

Cran pulled a weathered cloth bundle from under the table and slid it across. "Inside is a low-end burner, a couple hundred afghanis, and some food. Use the phone sparingly—one ping too many and we're all toast."

Afsar stood. "Understood."

He stepped into the back room, the tin door creaking slightly as it swung shut behind him. Inside, the air was cooler, the walls hung with spare garments, dusty maps, and a rusting cot. He stripped off his jeans and t-shirt and pulled on the loose-fitting, sun-faded shalwar kameez Cran had laid out for him earlier. It smelled of desert wind and old cedar. He wrapped the scarf around his neck and head in the regional Pashtun style, glancing into a cracked mirror on the wall.

When he stepped back out into the main room, Cran gave a low whistle. "You look like you belong here."

Chief handed him a worn satchel. "Stay sharp. Blend in. Listen more than you speak."

Afsar gave a small nod, eyes steady. "I'll see you both in two days."

Cran fished the Corolla's keys out of his pocket and gave them a spin on his finger before tossing them across the room. Afsar snatched them mid-air.

"Try not to get it blown up," Cran said with a smirk. "I just got the alignment fixed."

Afsar grinned faintly. "I'll try to bring it back with all four wheels."

Chief handed him a small, folded map with a red X marked on the outskirts of Spera. "Follow this route. Stay off the main roads where you can. There's an old mud-brick safehouse we've used before. You'll have a place to lay low and observe. Don't get too comfortable—it's a ghost shell with a bucket for plumbing and rats for roommates."

"Sounds better than the shack," Afsar quipped.

Chief raised a brow. "You'll be eating dates and dried goat by morning. You'll miss our shack."

They all chuckled, the humor thin but grounding. Afsar gave them a final nod, slung the satchel over his shoulder, and stepped outside. The Corolla sat under a tattered tarp in the makeshift garage. He peeled it off, climbed in, and started the engine. It coughed once, twice—then rumbled to life.

He backed out carefully as Cran pulled open the tin panel door and saluted lazily.

"Godspeed, kid," Cran called as the Corolla rolled past. "And remember: walk like you belong."

The drive was long and hot. Dust blew across the narrow roadways, and every few miles Afsar passed herders moving goats or children walking barefoot with bundles of firewood. The scenery shifted gradually—flat scrubland turning to rolling hills, scattered farms, then tighter mountain passes as he neared Khost.

He kept to Cran's directions, dodging checkpoints by turning down irrigation roads and old Soviet supply trails. The Corolla protested with every bump but held together.

As the sun started to dip toward the horizon, painting the sky in muted oranges and dusty pinks, Afsar spotted the village of Spera in the valley below. Mudbrick homes clustered around a dry riverbed, smoke rising from a few rooftop fires. Children played with sticks in the dust, and old men sat on stoops sipping tea.

He rolled through slowly, avoiding attention. Just outside the main village square, he turned down a narrow alley, passed a rusting oil drum, and pulled behind a crumbling wall as marked on Chief's map. The safehouse was exactly as promised—half-sunken roof, mismatched wooden door, and a faded green prayer rug hung over the lone window.

He parked the Corolla behind the wall, killed the engine, and stepped out. The air was cooling fast. Crickets had begun to sing.

Inside the safehouse, the air smelled of dust and old clay. Afsar dropped his satchel and sat on the floor, listening.

Afsar shut the warped wooden door behind him and slid the iron bolt across, listening for the satisfying *clunk* as it locked in place. He moved to the narrow window, lifted the faded prayer rug just enough to peek outside, and scanned the alley. Empty. Quiet. Just the low hum of evening life in the village.

He moved quickly through the one-room space, checking the corners, tapping along the walls for anything suspicious. Nothing but cracked mud-brick and timeworn silence.

Satisfied, he grabbed a small pack from his satchel and plopped it onto the floor. "Beef stew surprise," he muttered, pulling out an MRE and shaking his head. "Some things never change."

He activated the heating pouch, slid the meal inside, and waited as steam hissed softly in the cramped space. When it was ready, he tore it open and dug in, chewing slowly, his mind already running through tomorrow's objectives.

Across the room, he laid out a thin mat and unrolled his scarf to use as a pillow.

"Recon starts at dusk," he murmured to himself, brushing a layer of dust off the mat before lying down. "Sleep now. Work later."

As he closed his eyes, the distant sound of a dog barking echoed through the valley. Afsar didn't move. He let the exhaustion settle in, his breathing slow and steady, every muscle readying itself for the mission ahead.

Chapter 13

Afsar woke to the sound of wind scraping dust across the windowsill, the late afternoon sun casting a reddish hue through the cracked glass. He sat up slowly, taking a moment to reorient himself. The room was still, the only sound his own measured breathing.

He reached into his bag and pulled out another MRE, this time tearing into a packet of chicken and noodles. It wasn't much, but it'd fuel him long enough to get through the night. As he chewed, he laid out the folded map Cran had marked up earlier. He smoothed it across the floor, weighing the corners down with the empty MRE pouch and his canteen.

"All right," he muttered, running a finger along the main road that cut through Spera. "South alley runs along the old brick wall, here… market sits off-center, near the mosque… and these—"

He tapped four circles drawn in red ink, each representing a possible location the hostages could be held.

"Compound A, isolated, northern edge of the village. B, deeper inside, but higher walls. C has line of sight to the road. D's close to the well—too public?"

He committed each location to memory—approach angles, cover points, and exit routes. It wasn't just about observation; it was about survival. Blend, move, vanish.

Afsar rolled up the map and slipped it back into his satchel, already dressed in his shalwar kameez and scarf. He tied the scarf loosely around his neck, then looped it up over his head, casting a shadow across his features.

He glanced at himself in the small, tarnished mirror hanging by the door. The man who looked back didn't resemble the American agent who'd left Langley two days ago. This man belonged here—or at least looked like he did.

He slung the small satchel over his shoulder, double-checked the contents, and whispered, "Showtime."

Sliding the bolt back slowly, he eased the door open and stepped into the dusky evening light, one more face in the village of Spera.

Afsar slipped into the crowd like a drop of dye into water—unnoticed, absorbed by the flow of people weaving through the narrow market street. Evening prayers had just ended, and the stalls were buzzing with activity: spices in burlap sacks, pots of stewed lamb, children darting between carts, women haggling over bolts of fabric.

His scarf shaded most of his face, and he kept his posture relaxed, his gait unhurried. Just another villager moving through his evening routine. He approached the first target—a squat, aging structure pressed against the edge of the market square.

Afsar stopped near a vendor selling pomegranates, feigning interest as he leaned in and muttered to the vendor, "Baha chend ast?"

"Yek kilo—si rupiya," the man replied, offering a slice to taste.

Afsar nodded, taking the wedge with a polite smile and turning slightly to glance at the compound behind him.

The building was ordinary—sun-faded clay walls, a rusted gate leaning slightly off its hinges, and laundry flapping lazily on a line above the inner courtyard wall. A handful of older men were seated out front sipping chai, watching the world pass by. A pair of boys kicked a deflated ball near the side wall. There were no visible guards, no blocked-off alleys, no barred windows.

He moved down a few stalls, getting another angle from behind a curtain of hanging rugs.

No perimeter watch. No foot traffic in or out besides locals. Too exposed, he thought. *Not a chance they'd stash hostages here.*

Afsar glanced at the fading sun. He murmured low, almost to himself, "Strike one. Three more to go."

He turned from the market, tucking the last of the pomegranate into his mouth as he drifted deeper into the village's winding heart.

The northern edge of Spera had a different feel than the market. Fewer vendors, more dust. The sun had dipped below the jagged hills, casting long shadows that made the narrow streets feel tighter than they were.

Afsar moved slowly, hands tucked behind his back in the idle stance of a curious wanderer. His eyes tracked everything without ever appearing to fixate. The three-story building loomed ahead—newer construction than its neighbors, with concrete siding and barred windows. Its flat roof held a squat water tank, silhouetted against the dusk.

He crossed the street once, then again. On his third pass, he stopped at a tiny shop two doors down, where a boy no older than ten stood over a sizzling skillet of kebabs.

"Khushbu khub ast," Afsar said, smiling at the boy.

The kid grinned back proudly. "Chand migiri?"

"Yek," Afsar replied, handing over a few coins. He took the kebab and leaned against the shop wall, biting into it as he glanced up the block toward the target building.

A single man guarded the front door—mid-thirties, maybe older—with a Chinese knockoff of a Kalashnikov resting across his lap. He looked half-bored, barely acknowledging the steady stream of foot traffic coming and going. Young men, old men, a woman in a dusty chador, even a teenager in a school uniform.

Afsar chewed slowly, eyes narrowing.

Way too much civilian traffic. No checkpoint. No watch rotation. One guy with a rifle and no discipline. This is a flophouse or maybe a boarding home—not a holding site.

He crossed the street again, this time veering down a narrow side alley that looped behind the building. The rear was just as unassuming: laundry lines, a dog scratching itself near a trash pile, and a cracked door propped open with a rock.

Afsar muttered to himself as he walked away, blending into the dusk, "Strike two. Whoever's running this op isn't trusting a place like that with international hostages."

He wiped his hands on a rag and stuffed it in his pocket. Two down. Time to move.

Afsar moved quietly through the dimming streets, his scarf pulled a bit higher as the wind picked up. The third location sat hunched on the eastern edge of Spera, away from the bustle, perched where the town began giving way to rock and scrubland.

He approached from the south, using the shadow of a crumbling stone wall to screen his profile. From a distance, the building looked older—mud brick reinforced with concrete patches, high walls surrounding a central structure, and a rusted iron gate pulled shut. A single wire ran from a utility pole to the rooftop, but no light showed through the windows. No music. No conversations. Silence.

Afsar crouched behind the low wall, observing.

"No guards visible… no civilians either," he muttered under his breath. "That's… something."

He adjusted his position slightly, peeking toward a narrow alley that ran alongside the compound.

After a few more minutes, he grumbled, "Too quiet. That can be good or very bad."

He glanced up and down the street. Sparse foot traffic. A teenage boy walking a goat, a man unloading sacks of flour down the block, but no one near the compound. No loitering. No kids playing ball in the street. Nothing. It was like people knew to stay away.

Still, he didn't have the angles he needed. No vantage point for a clean look at the rear. Too much exposure. Too open.

Afsar stepped back from the wall and headed into the shadows again, muttering, "Too risky to linger without cover. I'll swing back later."

He disappeared down a winding path toward the last target.

"One more to go."

Afsar crept along the narrow roadside, the sun fully gone now, leaving the village cloaked in the deep hues of twilight and shadows. The final target sat on the western fringe of Spera—a collection of four buildings, walled in with stacked stone and reinforced with metal sheets. Even from a hundred meters out, Afsar could feel it. His gut tightened, the same instinct he'd learned to trust during his training.

"This has to be it," he whispered.

He spotted them immediately—two men posted at the main gate, AKs slung casually but eyes sharp. A third leaned against a wall inside the courtyard, smoking. A pickup truck was parked at an angle outside, its cab empty but the engine still warm— steam rising off the hood in the cooling air.

Then he saw it—a shallow drainage ditch along the opposite side of the dirt road, overgrown with thick brush. Without hesitation, Afsar slipped down the embankment and nestled into the undergrowth, staying low, steadying his breath.

He pulled the compact night vision monocular from his satchel and pressed it to his eye.

"Let's see what we're working with…"

Through the lens, details sharpened. A pair of sentries on the rooftop, rifles in hand, each taking turns scanning the perimeter with discipline. Not the lazy kind of lookouts—these men were alert.

"Too organized for a drug stash… way too tight for a weapons depot. This is something else," he murmured.

He adjusted his position slightly, making sure his outline was masked by a patch of wild thistle. Over the next hour, he tracked movements—three more armed men came and went through the courtyard, one carrying a metal canister, another leading a mule.

Then, just before the second hour passed, he spotted it—two of the rooftop sentries exchanged places with fresh guards. One of the men in the courtyard passed his rifle to a replacement and ducked into the main building.

Afsar narrowed his eyes. "Shift change. Regular rotation. This place is active—disciplined."

He clicked off the monocular and exhaled slowly.

"This is it," he said under his breath, eyes never leaving the compound. "They've got to be in there."

Afsar gave the compound one last glance before backing slowly out of the ditch, careful not to snap a twig or rustle the brush. He kept low, slipping into the shadows that stretched between mudbrick homes and empty alleys, weaving through the outskirts of Spera like smoke. The village had quieted down; the market noise had faded, replaced by the occasional bark of a dog or a murmured conversation behind closed doors.

He moved with practiced precision, every step deliberate. When he reached the safe house—he ducked inside and secured the door behind him.

Tossing his scarf onto the dusty table, Afsar pulled out the satellite phone from his satchel. He keyed in the encryption protocol Cran had drilled into him before departure, then typed out a quick message:

TARGET COMPOUND LIKELY LOCATED – WESTERN EDGE OF SPERA – GUARD ROTATIONS OBSERVED – FULL DEBRIEF TO FOLLOW – RETURNING ASAP.

He hit send, waited for the encrypted ping of confirmation, then set the device aside with a tired sigh.

"Time to get off my feet," he muttered, dragging his bedroll over near the corner where the cracked wall offered the best cover.

As he lay down, the adrenaline slowly faded, replaced by the dull throb of exhaustion in his limbs. He exhaled deeply, letting his eyes drift shut.

Chapter 14

The first light of dawn had just begun to spill over the jagged ridgelines surrounding Spera when Afsar slipped out of the safe house, dressed once again in his neutral-toned shalwar kameez. The air was crisp, filled with the faint smell of dust and smoke from early morning cook fires. He kept his head low, his pace casual but purposeful as he navigated the narrow dirt lanes of the village, retracing the same route he had taken days before.

The Corolla sat where he left it, half-concealed behind a slanted patch of fencing and an abandoned cart. Afsar gave it a once-over—nothing looked tampered with—then climbed in and started the engine, the rattle of the old car echoing off the stone walls nearby. He pulled out slowly, making his way past shuttered shops and early risers hauling crates of produce to market.

The road back to Kabul stretched long and barren, winding through valleys and along crumbling mountain passes. Four hours of solitary driving gave Afsar too much time to think—about the hostages, the compound, the weight of what came next. His mind flipped through every detail he had observed, replaying sentry positions, patrol intervals, and the layout of the target location like a mental tape loop.

It was nearly midday by the time he crossed into the outskirts of Kabul. The bustle of the capital hit like a wave—markets alive with shouting vendors, children darting between cars, trucks choking the roads in both directions. Afsar kept his head down and followed the turns Cran had mapped out for him until he reached the side alley that led to the safe house.

He pulled into the makeshift garage, killed the engine, and stepped out. The old tin door groaned as he slid it shut behind him.

The moment he entered the shack, the familiar smell of dust, oil, and reheated chai hit his nose. Afsar exhaled—he was back at base camp.

Afsar stepped into the main room, greeted by the low hum of a beat-up fan oscillating in the corner and the clatter of metal on ceramic. Cran stood over the stove, which they called the portable eye they used for cooking, poking at something in a dented pot while Chief leaned back in a rickety chair, sipping chai from a chipped mug.

"Well look who decided to come home," Cran grinned, not turning around. "Didn't get blown up, I see."

"Corolla's intact," Afsar said, tossing his bag onto the floor beside the table. "Figured you'd want that back in one piece."

"Damn right I do," Cran replied, scooping a ladleful of reheated lentils into a bowl. "This bucket's survived more warzones than most of Langley's desk jockeys."

Chief looked up and gave Afsar a nod. "How was the drive?"

"Uneventful," Afsar said, taking a seat across from him. "But dusty as hell. I forgot how much sand can work its way into everything."

Cran slid a bowl toward him and dropped two half-burnt flatbreads beside it. "Gourmet as ever," he said with a wink. "Lukewarm lentils and stale bread—fit for field royalty."

Afsar picked up the spoon and gave the food a quick stir. "After MREs, this is five-star."

Chief chuckled, cradling his mug. "He's officially broken in."

Cran grabbed his own bowl and sat down at the table. "So," he said between bites, "you going to make us beg for the good stuff, or you ready to debrief?"

Afsar smirked. "Let me finish chewing first. I've been thinking about this plate of lentils for the last twenty kilometers."

Chief set the bowls in the sink while Cran wiped off the small table with a threadbare rag. Afsar leaned against the counter, arms crossed, waiting until the clatter of dishes died down.

"All right," he started, voice steady. "I checked out all four locations like we planned. First spot? Complete wash. Too close to the market, no security, no patterns. Just a regular family compound with too many eyes on it."

Cran grunted, tossing the rag over his shoulder. "Knew it was a long shot."

Afsar nodded. "Second one was a three-story on the north edge. Had a guy with a rifle at the front door, but people were going in and out constantly. Kids, old men, women. No way they'd hold hostages there— too exposed, and no real control over access."

"Probably a boarding house or a local clinic," Chief said, drying his hands with a towel. "That's two down."

Afsar shifted his weight, the emerging soldier in him fully engaged now. "Third one had potential. Eastern edge of town. Low lights, isolated, not much movement. But too quiet. Couldn't get close enough for a proper assessment without drawing attention."

Cran scratched his beard. "Could still be in play. But you don't sound convinced."

"I'm not," Afsar replied. "Not after the fourth spot."

Both men paused and looked at him. Afsar's tone had changed—sharper, more sure.

"It's a compound of four buildings on the western outskirts," he continued. "Guards out front with AKs. Saw at least two on the rooftop during my recon. They rotated shifts like clockwork, every two hours. No foot traffic, no women or children coming or going. Whole place was locked down."

Chief's brow furrowed. "Did you get a read on their comms or signaling?"

"No radios that I could see, but they were using hand signals between posts. Well-disciplined. Not your average village militia."

Cran folded his arms. "Sounds like our jackpot."

"I think so," Afsar said. "The layout's tight, but there's a drainage ditch across the road with good cover. I watched the compound for five hours— never once did they break pattern."

Chief gave a low whistle. "Professional and cautious. Hostages are in there."

Cran nodded slowly. "Then we've got our target. Time to start planning."

He looked at both men. "We hit this right, no one hears a damn thing until we're already gone."

Afsar met his gaze, resolute. "Then let's get to work."

The map of Spera lay open on the table, corners weighted down with mugs and a rusted multi-tool. Cran traced the roads and buildings with a calloused finger while Chief laid out a clean white cloth and began assembling the FN MK 20 SSR with the slow, deliberate precision of someone who had done it a thousand times.

"All right," Cran began, "this is how it goes down."

Afsar leaned in, eyes scanning the details with a calm intensity. Chief just nodded, tightening the scope on the rifle.

"Chief, you'll be on the rooftop of the safe house— same one Afsar stayed in," Cran said, tapping the map. "It's got the best line of sight to the compound's roof."

Chief glanced up from his rifle. "Rooftop snipers first?"

"Exactly," Cran confirmed. "You drop the two on the roof clean. Quiet and fast. Then take out the ground sentries—pick 'em off before they can call for help. We need the compound blind before Afsar makes a move."

Chief gave a slight nod and went back to checking the rifle's bolt.

Afsar spoke next. "I'll already be in the ditch across the road, same spot I used for surveillance. Once Chief gives me the signal—two flashes from the mirror—I'll move."

"You breach the compound," Cran added, "eliminate any remaining threats, find the hostages, and clear the building. Fast and silent."

"And you?" Afsar asked.

Cran cracked a grin. "I'll be rolling up in the Land Cruiser the second you give the extraction signal. Doors open, engine hot. We load up the hostages and get the hell out of there."

He pointed at a narrow road behind the compound. "There's a service road that wraps around the western side. I'll come in from there—less exposure."

"And me?" Chief asked without looking up.

"You'll exfil back in the Corolla," Cran said. "Low profile. Head east through the secondary route and meet us back at base camp. No heroics."

Chief smirked. "No promises."

Afsar looked between the two men. "It's a tight window. If anything goes off-script—"

Cran cut in. "Then you improvise, adapt, and overcome. But we keep comms tight, stick to the plan, and no cowboy moves. We do this clean, we all walk away."

The room fell quiet for a moment, the weight of what was coming settling over them.

"Gear up," Cran said finally. "We move in two."

The safe house buzzed with quiet urgency as the three men packed in silence, the air thick with anticipation. The sound of zippers, the click of mags being loaded, and the soft thump of gear hitting duffel bags filled the room like a ritual drumbeat.

Chief slid a loaded mag into the MK 20 SSR and gave it a firm pat. "Three extra mags in the pouch. Suppressor's tight. Scope's zeroed for two-fifty."

Cran nodded, tossing him a folded shemagh. "You'll want this up top. That roof's sun-blasted during the day. Keeps the glare off your face."

Chief caught it without looking. "Always thinking of my complexion."

"Just don't sunbathe," Afsar muttered with a small grin as he strapped a knife to his ankle and pulled the strap snug.

Cran lifted a heavy black case from the floor and popped the latches. Inside was a suppressed sidearm, a suppressed Sig Sauer 225, smoke canisters, and a small bag of breaching charges. "You're good with the same loadout, Afsar?"

Afsar gave a single nod, checking the gun and pulling back the bolt. "Yeah. I want to keep it light. I'll be fast on foot once I'm inside. Sig's my friend."

Chief looked over. "Don't forget the signals. Radio silence after the initial go unless everything goes sideways."

"Got it." Afsar tightened the strap on his chest rig and slung the rifle over his shoulder.

Cran zipped up the last bag and hoisted it over his shoulder. "Land Cruiser's gassed and staged two blocks out, covered under that rusted-out tarp. We roll in thirty. Get your heads right."

Afsar gave the room one last glance before grabbing the sat phone and stuffing it into his pack. "It's time."

Chief slung his rifle and adjusted the strap on his scope bag. "Let's go bring them home."

No one said anything more.

Under the pale wash of early afternoon sunlight, the quiet clang of metal doors and shuffling boots echoed in the alley behind the safe house. Dust swirled low to the ground as the men made their final checks.

Chief dropped his gear into the Corolla's back seat, adjusting the rifle case wedged diagonally beside the passenger seat. He leaned on the roof and looked across the lot.

"You boys better not make me wait long," he said, a wry grin playing on his face.

Cran opened the back of the armored Land Cruiser and secured the duffels in place. "You'll have a view of the whole party from the roof. Try not to get too comfortable up there."

Chief gave him a small salute before slipping behind the wheel. The Corolla gave a soft sputter as it started, headlights remaining off. He pulled away slow, disappearing around the corner without another word.

Afsar stepped up to the passenger side of the Land Cruiser, resting one hand on the door handle, the other gripping the strap of his rifle. "Let's get this done."

Cran climbed into the driver's seat and glanced over. "You sure you're ready?"

Afsar buckled in without hesitation. "I've been ready since I saw their faces on that news feed."

Cran nodded once, then turned the ignition. The diesel engine grumbled to life. He rolled down the window and spat out a sunflower seed. "All right then. Let's go raise some hell."

With a slow press of the accelerator, the Land Cruiser rumbled out onto the empty road, the city fading in the rearview as they set their course toward Spera.

Chapter 15

The sun was sinking low behind the rugged ridgelines surrounding Spera, casting long orange shadows over the dusty roads as the Land Cruiser rolled to a stop in front of the safe house. The familiar corrugated tin glinted in the fading light like a tired sentinel, and the structure itself—barely worthy of being called a building—stood silent, just as Afsar had left it.

Chief's Corolla was already parked a block away, half-concealed behind a crumbling wall and a stand of scrub brush. He would be perched on the flat roof of the safe house, rifle bag open, the long barrel of the FN MK 20 SSR catching a glint of sun as he checked its scope one last time.

Cran stepped out of the Land Cruiser and stretched with a low grunt, his back popping in protest. "Never thought I'd miss the dust and stink of this place, but here we are again."

Afsar was already opening the back, lifting out his gear with quiet efficiency. He pulled on his chest rig and checked his sidearm, then glanced at the horizon.

"We've got about twenty minutes before full dark," he said. "Just enough time to get ready to get in position."

Chief's voice was calm and clipped. "Visibility's perfect. I will get eyes on the compound."

"Good," Afsar replied, slamming the back door shut. "We stick to the plan. We don't improvise unless it goes sideways."

Cran adjusted the rearview mirror and stepped back toward the driver's seat. "I'll be ready to roll the second you signal. You pull those people out of there, and I'll be waiting with the engine running."

Afsar nodded, pulling the scarf over his nose and tightening it behind his head. His eyes flicked to Chief one last time.

"Watch over us."

Chief gave a slight nod, already settling onto the roof, eye pressed to the scope.

With weapons checked and silence between them, the men turned to the dying light—every step forward drawing them closer to the mission's end.

Afsar crouched beside the Land Cruiser, fingers running over each piece of gear like a ritual. He popped open the small canvas pouch on his belt and double-checked the comms gear—earpiece, mic, spare battery—all good. His hand moved to the Ka-Bar knife strapped inside his waistband. Secure.

He drew the Sig Sauer P225 from his thigh holster and gave it a final look in the fading light. Smooth action, full mag. He pulled off his perhan turban, carefully tucked the weapon inside, and wrapped the cloth back around his head, securing it with a firm tug.

Cran leaned against the side of the vehicle, arms crossed, watching. "You sure you're ready?"

Afsar looked up, eyes calm. "If I'm not ready now, I never will be."

Chief's voice crackled quietly in his earpiece. "Clock's ticking. Two minutes until the roof goes dark."

Afsar nodded to no one in particular, exhaled once, then turned and slipped away from the vehicle. His boots made almost no sound on the dry dirt as he disappeared into the alleyway, his form vanishing into the deepening dusk like vapor.

Cran muttered under his breath, "Ghost in the wind."

From above, Chief's voice came steady and low: "Watch over him, God."

Afsar moved like smoke along the edge of the crumbling village, hugging walls and slipping through shadows as the last strands of daylight vanished. The air was cool now, the dry wind whispering through the alleys like a warning. He kept his head down, scanning every corner, every window, every rooftop.

The compound loomed ahead—a silent, brooding cluster of buildings etched in faint moonlight. Afsar ducked low and crossed the narrow dirt road, sliding into the ditch with practiced ease. The brush still covered the edge, just as it had the night before. He pressed himself flat, eyes locked on the compound across the way.

He reached up to his radio, pressed the transmit button once—*click*.

Back in the Land Cruiser, Cran gave a quick nod. "He's in."

On the rooftop, Chief adjusted the scope on the FN MK 20 SSR and whispered into the mic, "Copy that. Stand by."

Afsar remained still, blending perfectly with the terrain. The time for talk had passed. Now, it was just breath, heartbeat, and the hum of tension in the air.

Afsar lay motionless, barely breathing, the night vision monocular pressed to his eye. The compound was quiet but tense—like a coiled spring. He tracked the two rooftop snipers as they slowly shifted positions, rifles slung lazily across their chests.

Then—*thump*.

The first one dropped like a stone, his body crumpling against the low wall. The second didn't even have time to react before a second suppressed shot cracked through the silence and he folded backwards, arms flailing silently into the void.

Afsar's focus snapped to the ground-level sentries. One—*down*. Two—*down*. The third barely had time to turn before his knees buckled, a clean shot catching him center mass.

"Showtime," Afsar muttered.

He pushed himself up from the ditch and dashed across the road, his form a ghost in the moonlight. Dust kicked beneath his boots as he approached the compound's side wall. No shouting. No alarm. Just the crackle of a dying evening and the ringing silence of precision.

Afsar reached the outer gate, flattened against the wall, Sig drawn and ready.

Afsar took a slow breath, focused, and delivered a sharp, booted kick to the flimsy wooden door. It splintered with a loud crack, swinging inward on crooked hinges. He flowed in low, weapon raised, slicing the pie of the entry with smooth precision.

"Clear," he muttered to himself, sweeping the first tight corridor. His steps were silent, his breath steady.

He rounded into a larger space—a dimly lit living room with threadbare rugs and cushions scattered across the floor. Five men were just beginning to stir, blinking against the darkness and reaching for rifles propped nearby.

Too late.

Thppft! Thppft! Thppft!

The suppressor hissed with each squeeze of the trigger. One. Two. A third dropped before he could even stand. The fourth lunged for a weapon, and Afsar put two in his chest. The fifth managed a yell before a final round silenced him mid-shout.

Smoke hung low in the room. Afsar's eyes scanned fast—no movement.

"Living room clear," he whispered into his mic.

Without pause, he pivoted and moved deeper into the compound, slicing corners, checking doors.

Time was against him, and the hostages were still somewhere in the dark.

Afsar stepped into the narrow hallway, his suppressed Sig Sauer steady in a two-handed grip, muzzle leading every step. The compound had gone eerily quiet after the initial takedown. All that remained was this last stretch of corridor—and whatever waited behind it.

As he neared the final room, movement caught his eye. A slender young man, barely more than a teenager, stood in front of a thick wooden door secured with a rusted padlock, nervously fumbling with a ring of keys. His hands were shaking so badly the keys jingled in rhythm with his panic.

"Freeze! Hands up!" Afsar barked in Farsi, snapping his sights up on target.

The kid spun in place, startled, eyes going wide with horror.

"Dastat bālā!" Afsar repeated sharply in Dari, then again in Pashto—"Lasuna portah!"

The keyring slipped from the boy's fingers and clattered to the floor. His hands flew into the air like a puppet yanked by invisible strings.

"Please! Don't shoot!" the kid cried in a cracked voice, still in Pashto. "I—I'm not with them! I just bring food! I swear!"

Afsar advanced slowly, weapon unwavering, his gaze scanning for any sudden movements. "Step back," he ordered. "Away from the door."

The young man obeyed, trembling, backing against the wall with hands still raised. His face was a pale mask of fear, his chin trembling, mouth slightly open as if afraid to breathe wrong.

"Who's in that room?" Afsar asked, voice low and sharp.

"Foreigners. They're in there."

Afsar kept his weapon trained on the boy with one hand, bending down just enough to snatch the keys off the floor with the other. His pulse quickened.

"Don't move," he warned.

Afsar moved quickly but with practiced calm. Keeping his sidearm leveled, he reached behind him and pulled a flexicuffs from his cargo pocket.

"On your knees," he commanded the boy.

The young man obeyed instantly, dropping down without resistance. Afsar holstered his Sig momentarily, yanked the boy's arms behind his back, and cinched the flexicuffs tight. "Don't scream, don't move. Just sit here and keep breathing."

The kid nodded, terrified, lips pressed shut.

Afsar picked the keyring back up and turned to the padlock, flipping through the various mismatched keys, trying each one with rapid urgency.

Click.

The fifth key slid in and turned with a heavy clunk. The padlock dropped into his hand.

He pulled the door open cautiously, weapon back up and ready. What met him wasn't another room—it was a stairwell, steep and narrow, leading down into a basement.

A single, bare lightbulb flickered weakly at the bottom, casting long shadows on the concrete steps. The air that drifted up was stale, metallic, and faintly sour—like sweat, damp, and fear.

Afsar's eyes narrowed.

He looked over his shoulder at the boy, who now sat quietly, head bowed. Then he turned back toward the stairwell, exhaled once, and began descending, one careful step at a time.

"Let's see what we've got down here," he muttered under his breath, tightening his grip on the pistol.

Afsar moved cautiously down the narrow steps, each creak underfoot swallowed by the thick concrete walls. His Sig led the way, scanning every corner, every shadow. As he reached the bottom and turned the corner into the basement room, his breath caught for a moment.

Three figures sat huddled together on the floor, zip-tied and blindfolded. Their clothes were filthy, their faces gaunt with exhaustion, but unmistakable—he recognized them instantly from the Langley packet: the UNAMA workers.

Relief mixed with urgency as he holstered his pistol and drew the Ka-Bar knife from its sheath with a quiet hiss of steel.

"It's okay," he said in English, low but firm. "You're safe. I'm with the good guys."

One of the women flinched at the voice, then nodded slightly as the blade sliced cleanly through the first set of restraints. Afsar moved quickly, cutting through each zip-tie and helping them pull off their blindfolds.

"Can you walk?" he asked.

"I think so," one of the women said, blinking against the light. "Yes."

"Good," Afsar said, already pulling the smallest of them to her feet. "We move now."

He stepped back, keying his radio twice: *Click-click. Click-click. Click-click.*

Then a final burst of *Click-click-click.*

Cran would understand. *Target located. Three hostages. Moving out. One captive in tow.*

He turned toward the stairwell and glanced up. "Stay behind me. Move fast, stay quiet."

With that, Afsar guided them toward the light above, ready to exit the compound—and praying the path he'd cleared stayed that way.

At the top of the stairs, the young prisoner was still flexicuffed and seated against the wall, eyes wide and darting toward the basement door as Afsar emerged with the freed hostages.

"On your feet," Afsar ordered in clipped Pashto, grabbing the kid by the elbow and yanking him up.

The captive stumbled slightly but complied, his legs shaky, likely from adrenaline and fear. Afsar kept one firm hand on his shoulder as he led the group through the now-cleared hallway, his eyes scanning every corner for any last threats.

As they approached the front door, Afsar heard the familiar low growl of a diesel engine.

A second later, headlights swept across the yard as Cran rolled up in the armored Land Cruiser, keeping the engine running. The passenger-side door swung open.

Cran leaned halfway out the window and said, "You've got thirty seconds, then I'm punching it."

Afsar turned to the hostages. "Go! Backseat, now! Move!"

The three stumbled into motion, fatigue making their legs clumsy, but fear fueling their speed. They dashed across the dusty yard toward the Land Cruiser, ducking inside as Cran popped the rear door open for them.

Afsar tightened his grip on the prisoner's collar. "You're coming too," he muttered under his breath, half to himself, half to the dazed young man.

He gave the kid a firm push forward. "Go. Don't try anything stupid."

With his pistol drawn low and his eyes still sweeping the perimeter, Afsar followed close behind, guiding the prisoner toward the vehicle and the final leg of their escape.

Afsar shoved the prisoner up into the cargo area of the Land Cruiser with a grunt. "Get in and keep your damn head down," he barked, slamming the door shut behind him.

He turned to move toward the front passenger seat, boots crunching on the gravel, when—

CRACK!

The sharp whip of a rifle shot echoed across the compound.

"Ah—dammit!" Afsar staggered forward, clutching his shoulder as searing pain lanced through it. He didn't stop moving—he forced himself forward, adrenaline dulling the edges of the pain. He wrenched open the front passenger door and hurled himself into the seat.

Cran looked over sharply. "You hit?!"

"Yeah… shoulder," Afsar hissed, pulling his hand away from the wound. Blood was smeared across his fingers, hot and sticky. "Clean shot. Not deep, but it burns like hell."

He grabbed a rag from the center console and pressed it to the wound as Cran threw the vehicle into gear, tires spitting dust as they roared away from the compound.

Afsar's eyes scanned the ridge behind them instinctively. He froze, heart thudding—not just from the pain.

On a high ridge just beyond the village, silhouetted by the faintest moonlight, stood a lone figure. The glint of a scope caught Afsar's eye first, then the outline of an old bolt-action rifle. But it was the man's face that held Afsar's gaze.

Piercing, ice-blue eyes locked with his, even from that distance. The man didn't flinch. Didn't duck. He simply watched them drive away, rifle cradled in his arms like he had all the time in the world.

"Cran," Afsar said quietly, "I think we've got a new problem."

Cran didn't look away from the road. "Not tonight we don't. We're getting out of here first."

Afsar gave one last glance toward the fading figure on the ridge before settling back in the seat, still pressing down on the wound.
But those blue eyes… they stayed with him.

Afsar leaned his head back against the seat, his breathing growing shallow, the rag at his shoulder soaked through with dark blood. Every bump in the road sent a jolt of pain lancing through him. His vision blurred at the edges.

Cran glanced over, eyes tight. "Stay with me, buddy. We're almost there. You hear me?"

Afsar nodded weakly, but the world was already dimming.

The hum of the Land Cruiser's engine faded. The night outside dissolved into a fog of memory and darkness. Then, through the haze, warmth touched his cheek. A voice—soft, familiar, and impossibly gentle—broke through the quiet.

"Afsar-jaan…"

He opened his eyes. Not in the Land Cruiser. Not in pain.

He was standing in a sun-drenched field back home. Poppies danced on the breeze. And there she was.

His mother.

She smiled, just as he remembered. In her faded shawl, her hair tucked back the same way she used to do when making tea in the mornings.

"Madar…" he whispered.

She stepped closer, lifting her hand to cup his face.

"You saw him, didn't you?" she said softly.

Afsar blinked. "Saw who?"

"On the ridge."

His breath caught. "The sniper?"

Her expression darkened only slightly. "That was your uncle, my brother. I hoped you would never meet that side of our blood."

Afsar staggered slightly. "Why was he—why would he shoot me?"

"Because he walks a different path. One that leads only to sorrow." She touched his shoulder, right where the wound had been. No pain now. "But you must return, Afsar. Your father and Ashlynn need you. You are bound for important things that will help many people before we can be together again, forever."

His lips parted. "I'm so tired, Madar…"

She leaned forward and kissed his forehead. "Then rest… but only for a moment."

And just like that—
The warmth faded.
The poppies vanished.

He jolted back in the passenger seat of the Land Cruiser with a strangled gasp, blinking against the real world.

Cran let out a sharp breath. "Jesus, you scared me, man!"

Afsar coughed, then gave a faint smile despite the pain. "Tell Chief… we've got unfinished business… family business."

Epilogue

The wind carried a crisp bite as it swept through the open hillside, ruffling the hem of Afsar's long coat and fluttering the worn flags that lined the path to the cemetery gates. The late afternoon sun hung low behind a bank of clouds, casting a pale golden hue over the headstones beyond.

Afsar walked slowly, each step deliberate. His right arm was bound tightly in a sling, and thick bandages peeked out beneath his shirt collar at the shoulder. The wound still throbbed, a dull reminder of how close things had come. Ashlynn moved at his side, her hand gently braced beneath his good arm for support, her eyes fixed on the path ahead, respectful but watchful.

She hadn't left his side since he returned—navigating hospital corridors, late-night fevers, and the silent stretches of recovery when words weren't needed. She'd been a voice of calm in the whirlwind, and he knew he owed her more than he could say.

As they approached the rusted iron gate of the cemetery, Afsar stopped.

"This is as far as I go," she said quietly, sensing his pause.

He shook his head gently. "Yeah… I need to do the rest alone."

Ashlynn looked up at him, lips pressed into a soft line but nodded. "I'll be right here when you come back."

Afsar turned to her, his expression weary but grateful. "Thank you, Ash. For everything."

She gave his hand a final squeeze. "Go on, then. I'll be waiting."

With a breath drawn deep into aching ribs, Afsar stepped through the gate and began the walk among the graves.

Afsar moved slowly between the rows of headstones, his boots crunching softly on gravel and dry grass. He stopped before a worn but lovingly maintained marble marker shaded by a modest pine. The inscription, though faded, was still clear enough to read:

Afsoon Ramos
Beloved Mother, Wife, Friend
Gone, but never far.

He lowered himself gingerly, groaning as he crossed his legs beside her grave, the pain in his shoulder flaring before dulling again. He placed his hand on the cool stone, closed his eyes, and whispered with a soft smile, *"Salām Mādar. Man bargashtam."*

His throat tightened. He rubbed the back of his neck with his good hand, took a breath, and let the silence wrap around him for a moment before speaking again.

"You'd like her, you know. Ashlynn. She's... different. Kind. Brave. Funny in a very Western way. She makes this world feel lighter."

He chuckled softly to himself, then glanced toward the gate, where a faint silhouette of Ashlynn still lingered.

"She stayed with me every single day. Through the surgery, the sleepless nights, the fevers. When I was too weak to speak, she just sat there... held my hand, read from that terrible political novel I once said I liked."

His smile faded into something more serious.

"I think I'm starting to fall for her, Māmān. And it scares me. Not because of who she is... but because of who I've become."

He looked down, brushing his fingers along the grass that grew along the base of the stone.

"I wish you were here to tell me what to do. But I think... I think you'd tell me to stop running."

He let out a long breath, voice quiet. "I'm tired of running."

The wind rustled the pine overhead, and for a moment, it sounded like a whispered *"baleh."*

Afsar sat quietly for a few more moments, listening to the wind in the pine branches, his fingers idly tracing the grooves in his mother's name on the headstone.

His voice lowered, almost reverent.
"I saw you," he said, eyes fixed on the earth. "That night. In the back of the Land Cruiser. I was slipping—couldn't feel my arm, everything was spinning, and I just… I knew I wasn't going to make it."

He swallowed hard, his good hand curling into a fist in his lap.

"But then you were there."

He gave a half-laugh, one filled with disbelief and something close to awe.

"You looked the same. The same scarf you always wore on Eid, that soft smile that meant I was in trouble but you loved me anyway. You touched my face and said…" He paused, eyes glistening as the memory rose again. "You said the man on the ridge— he was your brother. My uncle."

His gaze drifted toward the sky. "All those years, you never spoke of him. I thought he was a ghost, just a whisper in the village. But he's real. Or… he was."

Afsar leaned closer to the grave, resting his forehead lightly against the top of the stone.

"Thank you for coming to me, Māmān. For bringing me back. I don't know if it was just the blood loss, or something greater—but it gave me the strength to hold on."

He pulled back and smiled sadly. "Even in death, you're still looking out for me."

The breeze picked up again, tugging gently at the sling on his arm. The pine branches swayed, whispering softly above him.

Afsar sat up straighter, adjusting his sling with a grimace before turning his eyes back to the headstone.

"I know what I need to do now, Māmān," he said, his voice low but steady, like a vow whispered to the earth itself. "I know why you showed me who he was."

His jaw clenched, and for a moment his lips pressed into a thin line, the pain in his shoulder now drowned out by something deeper—sharper.

"You can rest easy," he continued. "Because I'm not going to let this go."

He reached into his pocket and pulled out a worn photograph of her, the one she had taken the day before her wedding—eyes bright, a world ahead of her.

"He tried to take me from this world, just like he tried with you. Tried to finish what he started years ago. But I survived. And now, I'm going to make sure he never gets to do that to anyone else."

He set the photograph gently at the base of the grave, weighed it down with a small stone.

"You always taught me that justice wasn't just about revenge—it was about balance, about peace. But this…" He looked to the sky again, eyes hard. "This is about family. And no one betrays this family and walks away."

He stood slowly, wincing from the pull in his shoulder, but resolute.

"I'll find him, Māmān. And when I do, I'll finish it."

He placed a kiss on his fingertips and touched the stone lightly.

Afsar looked down at the headstone one last time, his fingers brushing the carved letters like he was committing them to memory again.

"Khoda hafez, Māmān," he whispered softly. "Tā baz didār — until we meet again."

A warm breeze rustled the dry grass around the grave as if the land itself was whispering back.

He turned and made his way slowly back toward the gate, his gait uneven from the strain, but his steps sure. Ashlynn stood there waiting, her hands tucked into the sleeves of her cardigan, watching him with quiet patience and soft concern in her eyes.

As he reached her, Afsar gave her a small, tired smile. He leaned in and gently pressed a kiss to her cheek— tentative, but sincere. The touch lingered just a moment longer than surprise allowed.

Ashlynn blinked, then smiled back, something unspoken passing between them.

Without a word, she opened the passenger door of her car for him.

He glanced back once over his shoulder at the cemetery gate, then turned to her.

"Let's go," he said.

And together, they left.

ABOUT THE AUTHOR

David Preston is a lifelong student of history and an avid reader with a passion for storytelling. With a background in Political Science from the University of South Alabama, he has spent his career navigating the worlds of politics, journalism, and business. A former politician and reporter, he now channels his deep knowledge of history and human nature into writing compelling historical and crime fiction.

Born in Gurdon, Arkansas, David has lived in Plano, Texas, and Hernando, Mississippi, before settling in Mobile, Alabama, where he has called home for the past 30 years. His novels, including *Unknown Soldier: World War I, 1828*, and *The Killer Family: A Martello Family Thriller*, bring history to life and deliver gripping, suspenseful narratives that keep readers enthralled.

Through meticulous research and immersive storytelling, David crafts novels that explore the past while delving into the complexities of human nature, crime, and the pursuit of justice.

www.ingramcontent.com/pod-product-compliance
Lightning Source LLC
Chambersburg PA
CBHW021036310726
48969CB00006B/1683